The Heart of the Sword
Shallin Awakes
Franklyn Thomas Jr.

Dedication

Jacklin Lindsey and Franklyn Thomas Sr, the two I proudly give thanks for my life. It is said in some places that a village raises a child, and I see my family as just that. Directly and indirectly, everyone in my family has played a part in my life, and for that I thank you all. There is the family that you are born with, and then there is the family that you obtain as you go along in life. As for them, they know who they are. You're the ones that gave me support, advice and true friendship, and for that I thank you all. There is one most special thanks that I must without a doubt bestow. If it were not for this person, I would not have seen my work worthy of completion. I was told that something could be made of my work, but I would have to be the one to make that happen. John Chanin put it in a way that was easy to understand. He simply said, "You need to finish what you have started." John, I thank you and I did just that. I finished the book and I will never forget the guidance you gave. In writing this book, I hope to take you on a quest through the mind and imagination of a boy, just a boy, who happens to look at the world in a different way than others may. If I am anything, I am Franklyn Thomas Jr, and, like Sanch, I am my father's son.

Foreword

In a land where the sword decided who lived and who died, came an almost unstoppable force. This force ripped through a once peaceful land. The beauty that once covered the hillside was now ravished by fire and the smell of death and destruction. Creatures that once lay dormant were now roaming the lands, leaving nothing but horror in their wake. Then, out of nowhere, a champion takes the lead on the battle to restore peace and beauty back to the land he loved more than life itself. Man had no chance until he showed himself. He and the men who banded with him brought peace back to the land, a peace that did not last long; an unexpected force that rose up and took the place of the evil that for a year had possessed the land. Once again this champion stepped up to bring this evil that, once again, threatened his people, as well as the land he loved and called home. *Its time was long ago, and still the battle lingers on as if it will last forever.*

The Heart of the Sword
Shallin Awakes
Chapter One

The noise as two swords clashed was like thunder over the land. It echoed off the mountains in the far distance and sent rocks crashing to the ground below. Nearer, Lackshin's young son, Sanch hid in the bushes, watching.

Lackshin fought fiercely as he swung Shallin —the only weapon known to give any hope of killing the one called Sillack.

Sanch held his tongue when Sillack's sword struck Shallin, then the smaller Lackshin kicked Sillack to the ground. The boy held his breath when Sillack matched his father's swing before he swiped Lackshin's legs from under him.

Although Sillack drew the battle's first blood, slashing Lackshin's sleeve, Sanch exhaled when his father rose to his feet, prepared for the next strike.

"He fights for his life and for the life of everyone in our village," almost escaped the little boy's lips, but he maintained his silent vigil. Though his father had never uttered the words, Sanch knew Lackshin would die, if it meant the others could live.

Even while blood dripped from his arm, Lackshin fought as if he had not been touched. He lunged at Sillack but Sillack's sword stopped Shallin from making her fatal strike. Lackshin countered, cutting Sillack along his chest.

Sillack roared and looked at the blood on his chest. "You? How did *you*–" He staggerd toward Lackshin with his sword raised over his head, but the more agile Lackshin dodged the powerful blow. Unable to escape Sillack's huge boot, however, Lackshin's view of the sky was blocked when his opponent stepped forward and straddled his fallen foe.

Lackshin positioned Shallin between himself and Sillack. The blades clashed and blocked the thrust long enough for Lackshin to stand. Still, Sillack bombarded Lackshin with a series of strikes. The injured Lackshin, weakened with every step, persisted in his response to Sillack's attack.

Sillack taunted, "Why don't you just give up? I can see in your sword that you
can't go on much longer. I will try to make it quick."

"If you want me dead, then kill me," Lackshin said. "But don't believe I will just lay down my sword and let you take my life. You might kill me, but someone much stronger than I will come for you. Know this. Shallin will accompany that one in the fight against you and the evil for which you stand. You *will* be destroyed."

Enraged, Sillack threw himself at Lackshin and knocked him off balance. Sillack
lunged at Lackshin, impaling him. With great effort, Lackshin stepped back off the sword, by forcing himself to step toward Sillack, the collision forcing the larger man to retreat. Lackshin's next swing with Shallin connected with Sillack's face. Sillack pursued Lackshin and cleaved his chest, while he removed the sword in one swift motion.

Lackshin and Shallin fell in death, as they had been in life, as one. A scream came from behind the crowd of people that had gathered.

Sanch ran out and a cloaked woman appeared and snatched the boy's hand. They ran off as if they knew nothing of Lackshin. Unnoticed, the woman and the stunned child hurried to safety in a village far away from the place they once called home.

Sanch did not see Sillack stand over his father's body. He did not see him turn to the crowd of people with his arms outstretched and his sword raised, but he heard him. "I am still here and he is no more. The one you called great is dead. I am now greater than he, his life taken by my hand."

Sillack reached down and picked up Shallin. He tried to speak strong words but Shallin's internal flame burned the palms of his hands. He said, "I now hold the sword of Lackshin in my hand. If any man dares to speak against me, let him speak now and face me." Unable to withstand the horrific pain Shallin inflicted on him, he threw the sword to the ground and ordered that none of his men touch the sword with their hands. "Destroy it! Immediately!"

One by one, Sillack's men attempted to remove Shallin from her master's side. Finally, four of his strongest managed to lift her with their own swords.

"It is strange," his captain said. "It is as if Shallin does not wish to be removed from her friend's side."

Once they lifted her from Lackshin's presence, they placed her in a sealed box and made her ready for travel. The men took Shallin to a place where swords were melted daily. When the swordsmith's hottest fire had turned to embers, the beautiful sword gleamed in the coals, undamaged.

They then tried to break the impressive sword
and were again unsuccessful.

"We must devise a clever way to destroy this
sword," one of the men said.

"Or else, we must find a way to dispose of it."
The captain scratched his chin and stared skyward.

Another of the men thought his plan would
surely work. "I have heard of a volcano that burns
hotter than any other, said to be the gateway to the
demon world. Some call it Hell's Doorway. We can
drop the sword into its heart. The intense heat will
certainly destroy Shallin, completing our task."

When Sillack's men dropped the sword into
the volcano, Shallin was pulled away by the
vigorous currents, pulled down toward the heart of
the volcano, and into an underground cave beneath
tons of lava. The currents pushed her onto a stone,
and from the lava, she became one with the stone.
Only her exposed handle received sunlight. The
lava still poured into the cave and the stone broke
loose from its floor. Again, Shallin moved, as the
lava pushed her, with the stone, into another section
of the cave, placing her on a hill formation, where
she found her resting place after a long journey
away from her fallen friend. A small hole at the top
of the cave allowed a fine ray of sunlight to touch
Shallin's hilt, allowing her some warmth, as well as
comfort, within such darkness.

She remained alone for six years, until Sillack
learned she still existed. He sent several of his best
men to the volcano where he thought the sword had
been destroyed...and almost forgotten.

* * *

"Mother," Sanch said, when she allowed him
to stop running, "why have we abandoned Father?

Why have we run so far? Why do we not go home?"

"My son, you are young. Not yet ten-years-old, and you cannot understand."

"I can try, if you will but tell me why you have forced me to run away."

Sanch's mother explained. "As long as Sillack or his men remain alive, we will never be able to return. I must be sure they cannot find us, for if they do, they will surely kill you and make me a slave to Sillack, or–"

"I will protect you, Mother. I know I am young, but I know I can protect you. One thing more do I know. I know that I will meet Sillack again. It is only matter of time. I will avenge my father, then."

As the years passed, Sanch thought only about finding Sillack, the man who killed his father. He spent most of his time training and preparing. He worked constantly to perfect his hand with a sword and he strengthened his fighting skills. In time, he became one of the best swordsmen in the countryside.

Eight Years Later

A young man stands in a fog-cloaked forest. Just beyond the tree line, he sees two red eyes, glaring at him through the mist. The man turns and runs. Behind him, he hears a horse galloping. Closer. Closer. The young man's courage returns so he stops, turns, and draws his sword. The creature breaks through the fog with the sound of shattering glass. Its eyes are bright red and blood drips from its mouth. The creature rears up and kicks the sword from the young man's hand, and knocks him to the ground. The beast hovers right above him, snarling. In the distance, the youth hears a familiar voice calling out to him.

"Wake up Sanch! Wake up! You're having a nightmare, again. It's only a dream, please, wake up," his mother said.

Sanch reached for his sword, but his mother gently touched his hand. She whispered, "This is not the time, but it will soon come." She held his hand as he eased it off the sword. "You will be ready, when the time comes."

"Mother, I think the time is now, for me to begin my quest," Sanch said.

"Do you truly feel that you're ready? I am concerned you may not be," she said.

"If not now, when? If I don't go soon, I may never find him. I know I'm ready. Do you think I can do what is required of me, Mother?"

"I know you can do this. You are Sanch, the son of Lackshin, the one who bears the right to hold your father's sword." She gripped his hand. "I believe in you."

"But, Sillack's men destroyed Shallin after he killed my father," he said "Or so go the rumors."

"Shallin cannot be destroyed by man. She was said to have been forged by the hands of the gods." A smile came upon her face.

"Then I must find her. Shallin is my father's sword, wherever she may be."

His mother put both hands on his shoulders. "Son, you *must* find her before you find Sillack." She gripped tightly, then allowed her hands to drop to her sides.

Sanch answered, "Why? I don't understand."

"Because," his mother said, "it's the only weapon that can kill Sillack. You *must* have her in your possession when you face him."

"But, where do I look? It was thrown into an inactive volcano, filled with lava. It can no longer exist, can it?"

"I told you, Shallin cannot be destroyed by any action from any man, so the volcano is where you must begin your quest." She insisted. "You must remember the sword you are looking for is your father's, and it *will* belong to you. However, the sword he wanted you to have is the sword I gave you when you were but a child, barely big enough to hold a sword. You must remember to be true to her, as well."

Sanch, could not return to sleep that night. As he lay awake he made one of the hardest decisions he would have to make. He gathered his things and left the village where he was safe, to find Shallin. He told no one he was leaving; not even his childhood friend.

Sanch stroked his horse. His firm, yet gentle touch calmed the huge animal that nickered at being awakened before dawn. "Quiet, my friend. Do you want to wake mother? We leave tonight, and depending on how things go, we may never see this place again. Either way, this is how it is to be. I knew this day would come." He pressed his face to his horse's chest. "I am happy to have you at my side. I will rely on your strength and companionship." Sanch, prepared for their long journey, walked him to the edge of the village.

Sanch rode all night to a town known to have been infested by Sillack's men. He hoped to move amongst Sillack's men and obtain information on the whereabouts of his father's sword. His

mother had spoken of a man named Thrant, said to
have knowledge of Shallin's location.

"Whoa," he said and leaned back. "We
should stop and rest for a little." He lowered himself
from his horse, where he stopped near a small river.
"We've been riding all night and we both need a
rest." He patted his horse as he dismounted and
looked toward his village. A dull orange sun rose
over clouds that seemed a dark blue from its shine.
"This is the first time in eight years we have been
outside our village."

He tied his horse to a small tree and fed him
an apple he'd brought from home. He whispered, "I
have a feeling someone is watching us. Keep a
sharp eye out while you eat this grass."

After a breakfast of fresh river fish, Sanch
led his horse near the opening of a nearby cave
where he rested until midday.

"Well, boy, if we are going to see this
dangerous village where Sillack's forces are
patrolling, we should get going. I think we'll walk
together. It's easier to talk to you that way." Sanch
made certain to leave no evidence he, or his horse,
had been there. "We're about to let the world know
Sillack can be stopped."

In the distance, he heard a woman scream
and his horse reared. "You hear that, too?" Sanch
released the reins and ran in the direction of the
scream. Close behind, his horse trotted, but did not
pass his rider.

As he got closer to the sound, he slowed
down to better assess the situation, and plan his

approach. Sanch saw a woman on her back, her torn garments strewn about. Two men encouraged another man attempting to have his way with her. Sanch stepped into the clearing, his shoulders out, his chest raised. Without word or warning, from his belt he pulled a dagger that was a gift from his mother, and put it through the neck of the first man he reached.

His companion heard the gurgling sound of blood escaping from his mate's throat and turned to see a smiling Sanch. "What the hell do you think you're doing, boy? Do you have any idea who we are?" He reached for his sword. "We are men of the great—"

With one motion, Sanch removed his blade and relocated it into the side of the approaching man's head. With his mouth still open, he fell off Sanch's dagger, still held firm in the young man's hand. With his other hand, Sanch reached for the man's sword and liberated it as its now dead owner fell.

"Now for you." Sanch held the blade of the dead swordsman to the back of the rapist's neck.

He stopped all movement.

The young woman pulled herself from under him and recoiled against a tree. She tried to cover her bloodied body with what clothing she could reach.

"Do you have any idea what you have done, and who you have done it to?" The man, still on his knees, asked Sanch.

"No, I do not know who are, but I do know what I have done and I am sure, from where you are now, you have an idea of what I am about to do." Sanch pushed the blade harder against the man's neck.

"Wait, wait, wait!" The man shouted. "What do you want? I have gold. I am able to give you whatever you want. Why kill me because of this whore? I can pay you and we can forget about all of this. You go your way and I go mine."

"She will be leaving with your gold and I see no reason to take your offer. I think I will leave with your life."

"Wait!" The man yelled, but Sanch did not hesitate. The man's head fell to the soft grass and rolled inches from its body.

"We should be going before the others come looking for them," Sanch said. "We must hurry."

The young girl rose to her feet and took Sanch's bloody hand. "This way. I live not too far from here. We will be safe there."

Sanch let out a soft whistle and his steed trotted from his hiding place.

"This way." The girl pulled aggressively on Sanch's hand.

"What were you doing out here by yourself?" Sanch removed a cloak from a sack on his horse and handed it to the girl who pulled it close to her body.

"I was taking a walk, as I have done many times. But in the past, I have always been able to avoid Sillack's men."

"Those were Sillack's men?" Sanch stopped walking. "Are there more of them around here?"

"Yes, they are always patrolling this area as if they are looking for something or someone." She pulled him back into motion.

"Where could I find more of those men?"

"Why the hell would you want to find men like them? They do nothing but rape, kill and take what they want." She released his hand. "Do not tell me you wish to join them, to be one of those monsters. If so we can part ways now! Thank you for saving me, but I hope never to see you again." She ran from him.

Sanch hurried to catch up with her. The cloak slipped from her shoulder when he touched her. He averted his eyes from her nakedness. "No, I do not wish to join them. I wish to kill them, all of them."

She turned to stare into his face. "Who are you?"

"Just a boy about my father's business. Now, how much farther to your village? I would like to see you home safe before I am on my way."

"Not much farther now," she said, as she reclaimed his hand, "plus, we need to clean you up before you head into town. They will surely ask questions if you walk in, looking as you do now."

"Thank you," he said.

"I should be thanking you."

When they arrived at her home, her mother ran to her side. "What happened?" She glared at Sanch and rearranged the cloak around her daughter.

"He saved me. He stopped three of Sillack's men from--" She looked back at Sanch.

"And then he insisted on making sure I made it home safely."

"What is your name, boy?" Her mother pulled the cloak tighter and brushed at her daughter's hair with her hand.

"My name is Sanch."

"Sanch, who?" Her mother asked. "Who are your parents? Where is your home?"

"Just Sanch."

"Very well, then. Now, let's get you both cleaned up before your brother and father return."

Water rolled off fingertips in large drops and Sanch fought the urge to look at the girl. He watched as the rag became pink from the soft mixture of blood and water, the cold water soothing and cleaning in its wake.

"Why is it you wish to kill them all," the girl said, When it did not look like you wanted to kill the three that you did? You do not strike me as a killer."

Silent as he cleaned the men's life-blood from his hands, he spoke only when the last residue had been removed. "I am not a killer. I am here to help those who need my–"

"But you *did* kill those–"

"I would have killed many more of Sillack's men, if it meant bringing you home safe," Sanch said, his eyes avoiding hers. "Tell me, please, the name of the girl I killed three men to save. You know my name, but I still do not know yours."

She took his hand, just as they heard a loud banging noise. As they turned toward the sound and Sanch rushed to stand, the water emptied at his feet.

"Father!" The girl released the young man's hand.

"Boy, come with me," her father bellowed.

With nothing more than a nod, Sanch followed.

"Helen," she whispered.

Sanch slowed his pace and dared a glimpse toward her.

"My name is Helen. I thank you for saving me. The gods must have sent you."

Helen's father laid Sanch to the barn where the smell of hay and horses filled his nostrils. Excited animals whinnied and nickered and the old man raised his voice to be heard above the noise. "How does Sanch, the son of Lackshin, come to be in my house? I thought your mother would do a better job of hiding you."

"How do you know who I am?"

"You're a lot smaller than your father was, but you look every bit like him. Judging by the story my daughter told her mother, you wield a sword like him, as well."

"You knew my father?" Sanch advanced closer. "How well did you know him?"

"As much as I would like to tell you about your father, there is no time. It will be dark soon, and you do not want to be in these woods after dark. The men out here tend to live without law, especially at night, and there will be more than three men for you to dispatch. Your horse is still saddled. We fed and watered him, so he is ready to go. You need to get going." Helen's father led him to where Aly waited.

"Will your household be safe when I leave? Won't Sillack's men make their way onto your lands and cause trouble?" Sanch asked.

"They could, but we have an understanding. They stay off my land and my son and I have no reason to kill them. Do not worry. Helen is safe now. She's home."

"Will you tell her goodbye for me, and to please stay out of the woods by herself?" Sanch turned and walk toward Aly.

"There are a lot of people still looking for you, Sanch. Some have waited long and suffered great pains waiting for Lackshin's boy to save them, and to bring a stop to Sillack's evil reign. Always remember, just like there are many who want to help, an equal amount wishes to see you dead. Sillack has taken from the good, and has give power to the worst. Know that some fight for him because they were given no choice and you may never truly know who your friends are or who you can trust. Find the ones being kept down by Sillack and you will find those willing to stand with you to stop him. We have waited a long time for the son of Lackshin."

Sanch found Aly ready to go. As horse and rider walked away, Sanch saw a curtain pulled aside, ever so carefully. He saw only a glimpse of Helen before the curtain dropped. He turned toward the sound of soft footsteps following him and smiled as Helen joined her father.

"Will he be okay, Father?" She gripped her father's forearm. "Three men are one thing, but a town full of them may pose more of a challenge for him."

"He should be fine." Helen's father moved the hair from her face. "He has a long distance to travel, and many people yet to kill before he finds what he seeks. We can not help him now, but we will be ready when the fight comes our way. I fear it will not be long before that happens."

At the edge of the nearest town, Sanch hid Aly until he had a room and somewhere secure for the horse to sleep. As Sanch entered the inn, he looked about for the man his mother had told him of many times.

This inn was a gathering place for Sillack's men and today, the normal, large crowd of people had congregated in the bar. Many were Sillack's drunk and unruly men.

Sanch sat at the bar and motioned for the bartender to approach. When the innkeeper leaned in, Sanch said in a low voice, "I need for a room for the night."

The bartender reached back and placed two glasses on the bar. He filled both to the brim and picked one up, motioning for Sanch to pick up the other. "You have a face I've seen before, boy." The man's glass still raised, he said, "To familiar faces."

Sanch held his glass without drinking. He glanced around, but no one seemed to have noticed the clank of the glasses touching.

"Drink up boy! You look like you have questions and the smell of this on your breath will make them more welcomed by the ones with the answers you seek." The bartender poured Sanch another drink. "As for your room, I'll go see what I can find."

Sanch remained at the bar where he had a view of the entire bar, much of which was new to his young eyes. He watched women pass from man to man, the older of them laughing and joking, but the younger women – even to Sanch's inexperienced perspective – were clearly new to their trade. He looked at the glass before him as he heard the splash of wine, the drunken talk of days past. Sanch took another drink and remembered his father's name, but not his face. The heat filled him and his chest inflated. A new face was enough to get the soldiers's attention.

The inkeeper returned and refilled Sanch's glass. "I found you a room, if you are still interested." He held his own glass up to assess its contents. "I should charge you extra. This is the good stuff."

Sanch leaned in and signaled the innkeeper to come closer. With the palm of his hand firmly on the handle of his sword, he asked, "Do you know a man named Thrant? He was said to have lived here some time ago."

"I do not know him. I'm just a simple innkeeper." The man started to walk away.

Sanch reached out and grabbed his arm. "Are you sure you have never heard of him? It is very important I find him. His name is Thrant."

The innkeeper pulled from Sanch, then grabbed the boy's shirt and jerked him close. His mouth almost touching the boy's face, he hissed, "Maybe, just maybe Thrant *is* familiar to me. I may have heard of him. Oh, yes, now I remember. He was the captain of Sillack's army and said to have had a hundred young boys killed in a nearby town. He was said to have ordered the death of Lackshin's son. Are you sure this is the right place to ask these questions? Look around you. Every man here can tell you where to find Thrant, but do you really want to ask them? Who are you, to be looking for such a man?"

Sanch pulled his shirt from the innkeeper's grip. His voice less than a whisper, he said, "I am the one they have been looking for, the one they were ordered to kill. I am Sanch, son of Lackshin." The young man sat taller on his stool and kept the old innkeeper's gaze. "This man, this Thrant, may have something of mine. I want it back, so I will ask again. Do you know where I can find him or should I ask one of these," Sanch turned and made as if to stand, "and make a mess of this place?"

"No need, no need," the innkeeper said with a smile. "You are indeed your father's son. I knew I had seen your face before. Sillack's men have Thrant in one of their camps. He is no longer the captain of Sillack's army, or the captain of anything, for that matter."

"Why is that?" Sanch asked.

"He stopped the death of someone Sillack wanted dead," the old man said, and refilled his own glass.

Sanch pushed his empty glass toward the bottle. "Who was this person and why did Thrant stop the killing?"

"No one knows who or why, they just know it happened and it almost—and may still—cost Thrant his life."

"I must find him. It is a matter of life and death for many people. Do you know of someone who will tell me how to find where Sillack's men are keeping him?"

"There is one who can help, but getting the help you need may not be a simple task," the innkeeper replied.

"Who is this person?"

"They all call her Lisha. She's well known, and trust me, you will know her when you see her. It should not be hard to find her."

"Her? A woman?"

"Yes, a woman. Do you have someone else in mind?" The old man straightened his back.

"No, but how is a woman going to help me?"

"You would be surprised." The innkeeper put his hand on young Sanch's shoulder. "Was it not a woman who taught you to use the sword at your side?"

"So, how am I to find her?"

"You're going to ask for her in the town. Then, she will find you. First, you must eat and rest. You will need to be in good form to search for Lisha."

"How can I sleep with Sillack's men in the same building? They will kill me if they discover my identity."

The innkeeper slid another glass across the bar and said, "No charge for the son of Lackshin." He gestured behind him. "Go through this door and climb the ladder you will find on the ground, to the second floor balcony. Once inside the middle window, bar the door. You will find food and drink waiting for you. Don't leave before sunrise. They will all be sleeping off tonight's drink in the morning. Tomorrow you may continue your quest to avenge your father. Tonight, you can sleep, assured of your safety, as long as I breathe."

Sanch did as instructed, and once satisfied in the security of the bar on the door, he walked back to the window overlooking the hill that separated his home from the rest of the world. He watched the sun setting behind his hill so far away, and farther still from the completion of his quest. Before he closed the shutters, he closed his eyes and the wind caressed his cheeks. He walked to the bed, sat down and placed his face in his hands. Then, he did what he always did when he came on hard times and needed inspiration. "Father, in your absence you have given me all I need to fight your enemies—my enemies—and to finish what you started. I hope I can do what even you were unable to do. Give me the strength I will need in order to do what is asked of me."

Before resting, he sharpened and polished his sword, in a vain attempt to remove a black stain from the blade. Once he returned his sword to its sheath and laid her on the bed next to where he would lie, he drifted off to sleep.

Chapter Two

When he awoke, he found himself no longer in bed, but in the forest and he sensed he was not alone. Something was in the forest with him, something ominous, and it was after him. He heard hooves, heavy on the dry leaves, and looked in the direction of the noise, but could not see what was coming through the thick fog. The wind swirled the fog and moved the rancid smell of the creature's breath into Sanch's face. It burned his nose. He looked deeper into the fog and two glowing red eyes glared back at him. He had seen those eyes before.

He turned to run, but his feet were strapped to the ground by vines that grew higher and higher. The eyes of the creature moved closer and they glowed ever brighter. Whatever it was, it smelled like death mixed with the rusty scent of blood. Sanch pulled his sword from its sheath and hacked desperately at the vines binding his feet. He pulled free and ran to put distance between him and whatever pursued. As he ran, he heard the gallop getting closer and closer. Sanch evaded his pursuer, but being born of a warrior, he could not resist the overwhelming urge to fight. The young warrior turned with sword in hand, ready to take on whatever was to come through the thick, blinding fog.

As soon as he stopped, the vines that held him earlier, returned to restrain him once again. As the gallop grew louder, the red of the creature's eyes glowed deeper and brighter. The warrior stood bound, but ready for whatever would come next.

Just as suddenly as he fell asleep, Sanch awoke, even before he could see his pursuer's face break through the fog. With his hands gripped tightly around the handle of his sword, he looked around. There was no mother to comfort the young man. He knew that he was truly on his own. He stood from the bed, sword still in hand. He walked over to a silver bowl, filled with water. The cold on his face, the wet awakening of the water was just what was needed. He looked at his distorted reflection. The sound of the drops returning to the bowl sent chills down his spine. He heard movement downstairs and walked over to the window. He looked out and saw a sunrise unlike any he had seen before. The sun crept over the hill in an amazing shade of red. Accepting this as a sign—a special send off, he thought of his mother and Unghell, the only true friend that he had left behind. Sanch did not tell him of his plans to leave because Unghell would have certainly followed him.

Curious about what or who was making the sounds, he tiptoed to the stairs. Softly he walked, to avoid detection because he did not know if friend or foe awaited him at the end of the dark stairwell. The more he descended, the more clearly he heard raised voices. One of the voices stood out, familiar.

Sanch recognized the voice of one of Sillack's men. He did not say much, but when he did talk, everyone listened.

"That boy you were talking to, who is he? I noticed he had a warrior sword." He pushed the innkeeper against the bar.

"He needed a room. He is upstairs." The innkeeper trembled as he spoke.

With his hand covering his face, Sanch stepped out from the shadow of the stairwell.

"I may have had too much to drink last night," he said. "What was in those bottles, barkeep?" He stumbled into the man holding the sword.

"Get off me, boy!" The soldier shouted and shoved Sanch against a nearby table.

"There is no need for that, my friend," Sanch said, as he rose to his feet. "I need a drink. Just water this time." Sanch placed himself between the innkeeper and the sword, and motioned the man to move behind the bar.

"Who are you, boy?" Sillack's man pointed his sword at Sanch's throat. "And what are you doing in my town?"

Sanch rocked back and forth on his feet, expressionless. "I am just passing through. The hour grew late and I decided to stop in this establishment for a drink or two. I was lucky he had a room for me as well." Sanch reached back to the bar to pick up his cup of water.

"And that sword. Where did a boy like *you* get a sword like *that*? That is the sword of a warrior. Did you steal it?"

Sanch drew his sword and before the soldier knew what had happened, his sword was no longer at Sanch's throat, but redirected and rendered useless.

"You mean this sword?" Sanch asked as he raised the cup and being refreshed by the cold of the water. "It was a gift from my father. I am not very good with it yet, but I feel like I may get a lot of practice in days to come."

Two other soldiers stood back having nothing to add to the conversation, their mouths agape, as their leader stood there without counter to this boy's sword.

"Come on there's no need for this!" Said with a quiver in his voice. The innkeeper knowing of the heavy repercussion that would follow if Sanch were to have killed this man. He grabbed the boy's shoulder; his grip firm in the way a father would manage his son. "Do not do this boy." His voice lowered to a whisper. "You kill him and his men will not stop until they find and kill you. We both know you have more important business to attend to." The innkeeper pulled Sanch closer and with his lips nearly pressed to his ear. "You are about your father's business young Sanch."

Sanch's stare narrowed and he lowered his sword.

"Why do you ask?" His head tilted and one eyebrow razed Sanch asked. Thrusting his chin at the solder "Your sword is nice as well. Where did you acquire it?"

He threw his shoulders back and shouted, "I am a soldier! This is the sword given to the ranking officers in Sillack's army, and you, boy, need to show respect."

"Oh, my apologies, sir." Sanch sheathed his sword. "I did not know my place. Again, I apologize. Please, give your lord Sillack my best. I hope to one day make his acquaintance." Sanch smiled broadly.

"I can arrange for you to meet him, now," The soldier replied.

Sanch turned around to the bar. "Another cup of water, please. "No. Today does not work for me. Today, I am seeing a woman about a sword." Sanch finished his water. "Thank you, innkeeper, for your hospitality." Before taking his leave, Sanch stopped in the doorway, "Innkeeper, are we good, here?"

The innkeeper replied, "I would say we are, young man."

Sanch turned and looked at the soldiers. "Are we good, here?"

The two lesser-ranking men nodded. Before the door slammed shut behind him, he looked to the senior soldier and said, "Keep practicing. You will get better with that sword." Then, as he walked out he shouted back, "'Till we meet again!"

Sanch walked a short distance to the stables where his traveling companion had spent his night. Like every other time, he was greeted by a head bump from his horse. "Aly, you would not believe my morning." Sanch gave his old friend an apple, and a good rub down before he started his search for Lisha in the town as the innkeeper had instructed.

Because he decided to walk, to keep his horse fresh, it took Sanch over three hours to arrive at the town where the innkeeper said he might find Lisha. Shortly after he entered the town, two men he had never seen before claimed loudly that Sanch owed them money.

"I do not know either of you, how can you possibly think that I owe you anything?" Sanch had to look up at the biggest man.

"That does not change the fact that you owe us money, and a lot of it. You'd better pay us or you are going to have some real trouble," the smaller of the men said, as they approached Sanch.

Sanch said, "I do not want any trouble. I just wish to be on my way."

The larger of the two men shrugged. "Well, pay us and you won't have any trouble. We can go on with our business and you can go on with yours."

"I don't think so. I do not owe you anything so I am not going to pay." Sanch's voice was low but firm.

"So boy, I guess you're going to have to fight us both."

"My name is not boy. It's Sanch, and if you two want a fight, so be it." He released the rein on his horse and Aly walked away.

The strangers pulled their weapons and strode toward Sanch. The smaller of the two had a sword, and the larger man wielded an ax the size of Sanch's upper body.

Sanch stepped back and drew his sword.

The bigger one attacked first. "This will be easy," he said, as he raised his ax high over his head and brought it down toward Sanch with a mighty force.

Sanch, smaller and faster than the man, dodged his swing. Then, with lightning-fast reaction, stepped on the ax handle and brought his knee up to meet the man's nose.

The man stumbled back with blood spurting from his face, but once again, he attacked. Sanch held his ground and defended himself with the sword his mother had said was a gift from his father. The young man countered with a move that lowered the weapon and gave him the opportunity to make a strike against the big man who struggled to raise his ax. A high swing spilled the large man's blood once more when Sanch cut his chest.

The smaller bandit attacked Sanch with his sword but was quickly thrown to the ground. Sanch prepared for their next attack. The big man with the ax growled in anger as he advanced.

From between two buildings, a firm, but soft voice said,

"Do you not think that is a little unfair, two against one?"

"I am doing just fine, thank you," Sanch shouted back to the voice.

"I still think you can stand a little help." A woman stepped from the shadows, ready with her sword.

Sanch glanced over. "Lisha?"

"Do I know you?"

"No, you do not know me, but I was told I would find you here."

The smaller man had returned to his feet and struck at Sanch's head, but Sanch ducked and brought his sword across the man's leg. He dropped his sword and grabbed his leg as he fell to the ground. The mad man with the ax charged toward Sanch, but Lisha positioned herself between Sanch and the attacker. She appeared to be dancing rather than fighting before she disarmed him and dismissed him and his limping friend, with a scolding but without any extra money and avoided eye contact.

"As for you," Lisha turned to Sanch, "who are you and how is it that you know my name?"

"I am Sanch, and I was told you would be able to help me."

"Help you with what?" She asked with her head lowered. Her cheeks tightened and her voice slightly raised.

"A quest."

She leaned and let out a laugh. "A quest of what kind?"

"A quest of great importance!" Sanch jutted his chin out and squared his shoulders.

"What makes you think that I can help you?" She asked as she slapped her pants sending a cloud of dust bellowing.

"I heard you are a good fighter and I've seen your skills for myself, though I did not request your help with my little skirmish. Will you help me or not?"

"Tell me more about this quest of great importance and how I am supposed to help you."

With his eyes fixed on the ground "I am looking for the man who killed my father,"

"Oh, that explains *everything*," she said. "Just what, exactly, do you plan on doing with him when you find him?"

"I intend to kill him," Sanch said. His eyes narrowed and the muscles in his clenched jaw tightened into a knot. "Just as he killed my father!"

"Who was your father?" Lisha asked.

With his chest inflated "I am the son of Lackshin."

"I've heard of him. And that would make the man you wish to kill–"

"Sillack."

Lisa asked, "So, that makes you..."

"That makes me Sanch, the son of Lackshin, the man who will take the life of Sillack. I grow weary of your questions, woman. I must be on my way with or without you. I will ask you once more, will you help me?" Sanch sheathed his sword with an exaggerated arm motion, making it clatter in its holder.

"I have more questions that you must answer if you want my help. What makes you think you can kill Sillack, even if I can help you find him and who told you about me?"

"Your reputation precedes you. I have heard of your skill with a sword and as I said before, I have seen you in action."

"You didn't answer my other question. Who told you about me?"

"Oh, just a friend."

"Does this friend have a name?" Lisha placed her hands on her hips and cocked her head to one side.

Sanch said, "You know, he never told me his name, although I did meet him in a town not too far from here."

"I am going to *kill* that damned innkeeper!" Lisha clenched her fists and shook them toward the sky.

"How did you know who it was?"

Lisha turned toward the town Sanch had just left and walked fast enough to stir up a small dust trail.

"Come on! You're going the wrong way!" Sanch hurried to catch up to her.

"No, I'm not. I am going to kill that innkeeper. He has a big mouth and

I am going to shut it for him!"

Sanch shouted and spoke with a crack in his voice, "We have no time for this! We must find Thrant before Sillack has no more reason to keep him around."

She kept walking but her pace had slowed, some.

Sanch said, "You can kill him the next time you see him."

Lisha turned and glared. "Okay, fine, the next time I see him, I will kill him. For now, I will go with you, but if I find that you are on a fool's quest, I am finished. You understand me *Son* of *Lackshin*?"

A smile crept across his face. "Yes, I understand. Okay, good. Can we go find Thrant, now?"

Lisha returned to Sanch and after studying him a moment, she said, "So, Sillack turned on good old Thrant. What did Thrant do, and does your mother know you're this far from home?"

"He saved the life of someone Sillack wanted dead, so Sillack put him in chains. At least, that is what I was told and you need not concern yourself with what my mother knows."

Aly had returned to Sanch's side and was nuzzling his shoulder.

"Who is this beautiful animal? Your horse?"

"No, this is Aly, my friend," Sanch replied as he stroked Aly's chest.

"Do you know this man Thrant? It seems as if you do."

"Of course. He and my father were in the same army. They were like brothers." she said. "I guess we should get going."

They walked to where Lisha kept her horse and soon they were on their way to find Thrant. After riding two and a half days and inquiring into the whereabouts of where Thrant was being held, they found the camp in a valley, but they were on the top of one of the smaller mountains surrounding it.

"Boy, that's a long way down," Sanch said.

"It is." She laughed.

"Any smart ideas Sanch, Son of Lackshin?"

He turned to her. "Not at the moment, how about you?"

She smiled and asked, "Do you, by any chance, have some rope?"

He shook his head. "No, but I'm sure if we look, we can find another way down."

Lisha, looked over her shoulders. "Yes, I'm sure you are right, but I forgot my wings, today."

"Lisha, are you going to be helpful or are you going to be a pain in my ass the entire time?"

Dropping her voice to a whisper, while batting her eyelashes, she said, "I'm going to help you, of course, but while being a pain in your ass." She winked at him.

Sanch chuckled. "That will have to do, then," he said. "So help me look for another way down." He looked around the area.

She said, "Why don't we just take the path down the side of the mountain?"

"What path down the mountain?"

"The one over there, on the your side of the mountain." She pointed to the path.

"Why did you not say that before?"

Lisha shrugged. "You did not ask me before, and besides, I figured you knew it was there."

"Exactly how would I know? Never mind," Sanch said. "Let's go. We don't have much day left, and we don't want to have to navigate that narrow path with so little light. And still we need a safe place for the horses till we return."

Sanch rested his hand on the handle of his sword.

"So, tell me," Lisha asked, with raised eyebrows, "what is so important about this man, for you to go to such lengths to find him? Why do you need him so?"

"He is going to help me find something I need."

Lisha said, "Well, that's vague. What exactly is it he is going to help you find?"

In a soft voice, Sanch said, "My sword."

"But your sword is in your damn hand!"

"Not this one, the one my father had when he was alive."

"What do you need with his sword? You have your own."

"Yes, but I need my father's sword to kill Sillack."

Lisha held her sword out to him. "Use mine."

Sanch said, "Your sword would not be able kill him. My sword will not be able to kill him. He is not like other men. In fact, he is not a man you can fight with normal swords. I need a sword forged by the hands of gods and steel of the same, cooled by the blood of my father. That is why I need that particular sword."

"Okay. Let's go. I just wanted to know why I was risking my life, and for what, that is all." she said.

He took a deep breath. "And I do thank you for that. I will repay you, I promise."

A smile returned to her face. "That is okay, I do not need to be repaid. The joy of making you miserable will be payment enough."

Sanch saw something moving in the bushes, so he signaled for Lisha to look.

"Over there, Lisha do you see it?" he whispered.

She strained to get a better look. "Yes, but what is it, what does it want?

Let's just go, maybe it did not see us."

"Yeah," He agreed, "maybe it did-"

Before he could finish, men with swords and axes ran toward Sanch and Lisha shouting battle cries.

Lisha said, "Sanch, can you actually use that thing?"

"Shut up and fight," he said, just as the leader of the onslaught called off the attack.

"I guess they have heard of me, too," Lisha said as she rolled her eyes and tightened her lips to hold back a laugh, "or maybe they know who you are, mighty Sanch, son of the great Lackshin."

Chapter Three

A large man approached Sanch and Lisha. His ax rested easily on his shoulder and he walked with the stride of an angry man.

"Great, another man with an ax," Sanch mumbled.
This man's words had brought a stop to the attack from the other men.

"He must be the leader," Lisha said.

The man stepped up to the warriors and looked them over before he glared down at Sanch and asked, "Who are you and what brings you to my land?"

Sanch's hand firmly rested on the handle of his sword. He looked the man fully in his eyes and answered. "I am Sanch. This is my traveling companion, Lisha. We did not know this was your land. In no way did we mean to disrespect you or your people. We are just passing through."

The man asked, "What business could you two have here on our land?"

"Not on your land, sir," Sanch said, "on that land, down in the valley."

The man paused, looked into the distance, then he asked, "What kind of dealings would you have with Sillack's men? They are evil, and they will kill you both — just for fun. You are making it too easy for them by walking down there. Do you not value your lives?" He stroked his chin. "At least make them do a little work to kill you. Let them come find you. Do not go to them."

One of the other men shouted something, sending the others into a laughing frenzy.

"Quiet!" Their leader shouted. But, he also chuckled a little. "Really, what do you plan on doing down there?"

Sanch explained. "They are holding a man captive, a man whose help I desperately need."

The leader looked around. "Where are your men? How many are with you?"

"It's just Lisha and myself."

"Do you *truly* plan on getting out of there alive?"

Sanch squared his shoulders. "What! Do you not think she and I can handle ourselves?"

"No, I do not think either of you will survive. Not long, at least. There are men with swords waiting for people like you to try such foolishness."

Lisha stepped forward, drawing her sword as she walked. "Yes, they have swords, but these are not sticks we are carrying."

"Look. You might need some help. That's all I am saying." The man stepped closer to them.

"Are you just telling us this, or do you intend to help us?" Sanch relaxed his grip on his pommel.

"I'm offering my help, and the help of my men, if they agree. My people and I hold no love for Sillack, his ways, nor his men." The man leaned in. "So, tell me of your plans, young man."

Sanch said, "We do not intend to start a war. We just want to pull this man out, alive. You and two or three of your men should be plenty. Lisha and I can handle the rest."

"But, have all your men close by, in case we do run into trouble," Lisha said.

"That's a good idea," Sanch said.

She shrugged. "I know. It was my idea, after all."

She looked at the leader and asked, "What do we call you?"

The man turned to her. "They call me Hannes and you may now also call me, friend."

Sanch took his hand. "Well, friend, pick your men and we will be on our way."

Hannes called three men by name, and told the others, "Stand ready, not too far from their camp."

They made their way to the bottom of the valley and waited for the cover of darkness, to hide their entrance, before they moved in to retrieve Thrant.

Sanch said, "Okay, we are going to break up into groups of two. Lisha and I will be one group. You and your men can decide, between the four of you, how you will team up."

One of the men asked, "What if we run into other prisoners?"

Hannes turned to Sanch. "My man has a point. What do you want us to do?"

"We take them with us. No one deserves to be imprisoned, and those we cannot take, we'll come back for, later."

"Okay, let's do this." Lisha started in the direction of the camp.

They moved out, like they were a part of the night, and just as quiet. They searched the camp as if their lives depended on success.

Sanch pointed to a small, heavily guarded building with a heavy door and slits for windows. "Lisha, look! Do you think they would keep him in there?" One man stood at the door and one was posted at either side of the building with another at the back.

"How do we even get a peek?" Lisha asked.

Sanch said, "The back of the building is not as well-lighted as the front and sides. That is how we will move in to get our look. I will take out the guard at the back, then you move around to the guard on the left and I'll take out the one on the right. We must move in quietly, so we aren't seen."

Lisha took her position behind her man and held it. Sanch eased into position, then in one motion, he grabbed the guard and with one quick snap, he broke his neck and lowered him to the ground. He motioned to Lisha, who pulled her knife and cut the throat of the guard on the left, making him unable to scream out. Sanch did the same with the guard on the other end of the building, then moved around and grabbed the guard stationed at the door. He put his sword to the guard's neck and told him, "If you wish to live, you will stay quiet and open that door."

"Yeah, you should do what he tells you." Lisha stepped closer, her own sword drawn. "He is a man on a mission and you do not want to get in his way. So do yourself a favor and open the door for the nice man with his sword to your neck."

"Okay, Okay, I have the key." The guard fumbled in his pocket.

* * *

On the other side of camp, Hannes and his men were also hard at work searching for Thrant. Instead, they found an unguarded pit where slaves were being held.

"Help us. Please, help get us out of here," someone pleaded.

"Be quiet. We will get you all out. Just keep it down so no one will hear you," Hannes' man said. "Where are the guards?"

"We have to get these people out of here before the guards return." Hannes ordered his man into action.

The young man accompanying Hannes noticed a lever and started to pull. When the lever did not move, he said, "Hannes, I think this is what opens the pit. Come, help me with it."

They exerted all their strength, and after intense pulling, the lever moved and opened the pit.

Hannes whispered, "Come on out, one at a time. We need to hurry, to get everyone—"

A young girl ran up to Hannes crying. "We have to save him! We have to save him!"

Hannes asked, "Save who?"

"My father, he is the reason there are no guards. They do not miss an execution. We have to save him! Please, hurry."

"We have to find Sanch and Lisha, first, then we can go to your father."
She looked at Hannes. "Are there are more of you?"

"Yes, we are here to find a man named Thrant. Do you know where we can find him?"

"Yes," she said, "but my father..."

Hannes said to his companion, "Take these people to safety. The others will help me find Sanch."

"Yes, sir."

"Return with all the men. I expect we will need every hand for the fight tonight."

* * *

A guard opened the door to what had, moments before, been a fortress. In the shadows, a man stood up and stepped back.

Sanch approached him. "Thrant, we are here to free you."

"And you are who, exactly?" Thrant asked.

"I am Sanch, son of Lackshin and this is—"

Thrant smiled. "—Thank you, son of Lackshin. Lisha, how you have grown. I thank you, as well." He walked from the shadows. "So, to what do I owe this honor?"

"You know of something I need, and only you can tell me its whereabouts." Sanch nodded toward Lisha. "How is it that you know my companion?"

Before Thrant could answer, Hannes and the girl arrived at the jail that was once Thrant's home. "We must hurry. This girl's father is to be unjustly executed. She needs our help."

Sanch asked, "Where?"

"She will show us," Hannes said.

They followed her until they came to an opening in the center of the camp.

"There. See. That's where all the guards are," the girl said.

"What do you mean," Sanch asked, "all the guards?"

Hannes said, "When my men and I found the place where the adults were being held, there were no guards on watch."

Lisha stepped forward and joined the conversation. "What do you suggest we do?"

Sanch said, "We are going to get that man out of there."

"How are we going to do that?"

"Hannes and his men will surround the camp."

Hannes asked, "Then what?"

"Signal me when your men are in position. Then wait for my signal."

"What are you going to be doing?" Lisha paced.

"Me? I'm going to say hello to those gentlemen," Sanch said. "You may stay here with the girl, if you choose. But, please feel free to jump in, anytime you're ready." Sanch walked right into the midst of the crowd of jeering men who were taunting the girl's father.

One of the men stepped forward. "Who are you and what the hell are you doing here?"

"I am Sanch—"

"—Son of Lackshin." Lisha stepped out of the dark. "That means you are holding a friend of his. I suggest you let him go."

When the laughter died down, one of the other men said, "Or what?"

An arrow flew threw the dark and pierced the chest of the man who had last spoken.

Sanch stepped toward their prisoner and said, "That. That is what. Any more questions?"

The man who demanded Sanch's name turned to Lisha. "Just one. Can he get to me before I get to you?"

She said, "He will not have to. I can handle you without his help."

Sanch yelled a guttural and visceral cry. "We don't have time for this! Just cut him open, Lisha! This need not take long."

His ax raised high, Sanch's new-found enemy charged and roared. Sanch's blade met the ax, and Sanch backed off, ready for his come back.

"You will die, tonight, by my ax!"

"Not if my sword has anything to say about that."

Lisha called out. "Sanch come on! We have what we came for. He's safe. Me must go."

"Oh, look," Sanch said, "it's time for me to go. I guess we'll have to finish this, another day."

"We finish now!" His opponent growled more than spoke.

Sanch took a step back, flung his left arm out, took a bow, raised his right arm to his chest, then raised his left arm. "Fear not. You will have your chance, for we will meet again."

Sanch disappeared into the night with Lisha, the young girl, her father and their other friends, including Thrant. "Who was that?" someone in the camp asked.

"Sir, he claimed to be the son of Lackshin," the wounded man said.

"The son of Lackshin was killed as a boy. Sillack will not be happy with this news."

* * *

In the dark, Sanch regrouped, with Hannes and his men, at their camp. "Now was that fun, or was that fun?" Sanch asked, with a grin on his face.

"That was not fun. You almost got killed!" Lisha shouted.

Sanch laughed. "He was good but not that good."

"It got the blood pumping, and my men needed a good fight," Hannes said.

"Thank you I knew you would see my point." Sanch slapped him on the back.

Lisha shook her head. "Men! You are made for one another."

Sanch turned towards Thrant. "Do you have any idea why we came to get you?"

Thrant hesitated, then said, "At first, I didn't know, but when you claimed to be the son of Lackshin, I knew you could only want one thing, Shallin, your father's sword. But I still don't understand how you got Lisha to come with you."

Sanch inquired again, about the relationship between Lisha and Thrant. This time, he turned to the woman. "It seems you two are old friends."

Lisha said, "No. I have never met him before today."

"But he seems to know you."

"Cannot you just leave it alone?" Lisha glared at him, then turned away.

"Fine. I will not ask again, since it seems to be a tender subject. Now, Thrant, can you help me find my father's sword?"

Thrant nodded. "I can help, but are sure you are up to it?"

Sanch smiled. "I can handle whatever is waiting for me."

Thrant looked into his eyes. "I hope so, because you are the only one who can get near that sword."

"Then I guess I have no choice but to be ready." Sanch patted his sword.

Lisha said, "I am sick of all the jabbering. Are you guys going to talk about it or are you going to do it?"

Sanch said, "I just want to be sure I'm ready. I need to know what I'm doing before I take one step near that sword."

"Now, you want to think through what is to be done, you who jumps into fights without thinking? Then, think and do whatever it is that you have to do. Let's be on our way." Lisha walked away from the men.

"I can tell you what you should know, on the way there, so by the time we arrive, you'll be ready," Thrant said.

"Good. Let's get some rest and be on our way at first light." Sanch turned to see Hannes approaching.

"One of my men wishes to join your quest. He told me that after fighting alongside you in the valley camp, he felt compelled to see the fight to the end, at your side." Hannes motioned to a boy, not much older than Sanch.

"I remember you." Sanch looked up to the man and stretched his arms wide to clap him on both shoulders. "Hannes chose you, first, to come with us. You cannot leave your people in times like we are about to see. They will need you at home." Sanch released his grip and stepped back, so he could see the man's face without looking upward. "As soon as the word makes it to Sillack that the son of Lackshin is alive, things in this world are going to change rather quickly. I'm afraid, not for the better."

"There are other men here, who are braver than I, who will protect the village," the young man said.

"I have yet to see one of those men, said to be braver than you. You know that I am Sanch, but I do not know your name. If we are to be traveling together, I would like to know the name of the man I'm sure will be given several opportunities to save my ass."

"They call me Menis. I will be honored to ride at your side and see you to your father's sword."

"This will be the stuff of ballads, something people will discuss for years to come. Yours is a worthy name that will forever be spoken with respect and gratitude. Now we need some rest after a night like the one we've all had."

"Yes," Hannes said, "and we still need to find bedding for those we freed tonight. Returning them all to their homes will be a task all its own, for another day."

"Then, we will meet again in the morning, when the real adventure begins." Sanch reached up and placed his hand on Menis' shoulder before leaving to find the tent Hannes had his men set up for him. Once in the tent, he lay there, looking at the patched-together fabric that separated him from the stars. He thought of what, with just a hand full of men, he had just achieved. He covered his face with his hands, ran his fingers down his face and thought of all that could have gone wrong, all the lives that might have been lost in his quest to find his father's sword.

The fire crackled like a hand crushing dry leaves, the logs popped like the loud snapping of fingers. Outside the tent, Sanch heard the sounds of celebration as the joy of the newly-freed slaves filled the camp. With those sounds, his eyes slowly closed and he drifted off to sleep, knowing he had done something right.

Wine poured over cups like an out-of-control waterfall. Men and women shared stories of previous battles and talked of plans for the future. Strangers became friends. Freedom returned to the deserving. Quiet finally reigned triumphant and many found peace in their tents. Dew fell throughout the night.

The ground appeared to have been scattered with diamond-like droplets of morning tears, as night retreated.

Hannes rose early to greet the sun, the victor over the night. "How was your night, boy?" he asked Sanch, whose head had emerged from his tent at the first sounds of morning.

"It was a good night. The thought of victory was like a sweet song to lull me to sleep. Are the others awake yet?"

"I think I saw that one called Thrant moving about this morning. I believe he left his tent to take a piss. As a newly freed man, some of the women took great care to attend his needs, last night."

Sanch stepped out of his tent. "Did you say *women*?"

"Yes. Who knows how long he has been without the soft touch of a woman? From the sounds inside his tent last night, he has made up for time lost. I'm sure you will find him back inside, now."

"Thank you. I hope I find him well-rested and ready to travel." Sanch walked to Thrant's tent. As he pulled back the flaps, moist with dew, he saw the man enthralled with one woman, as others lay about the tent, naked as the day they entered the world. "I do hope you were able to get *some* sleep last night. We have a long ride to make, today."

His presence did not give reason for them to cease their activities. "My boy, my boy, feel free to help yourself to the softer sex." Thrant caressed the ass of the woman who hovered over him. "Trust me they all have their specialties."

"When you are done here, you know where to find us." Sanch retreated from the tent and the heavy odor of sex and sweat. He stopped for a minute and looked up at the sky. He closed his eyes and let the last of the falling dew drop onto his face like the soft footsteps of butterflies.

"Son of Lackshin." Sanch heard the soft voice, louder than a whisper, yet softer than usual. Lisha. "Isn't it time to leave? I have had my fill of this place and I am ready to be on my way. Where is Thrant?"

A smile crept across Sanch's face. "He's saying goodbye to some new friends. Soon, he will join us and we shall begin. Now let's go find that mountain of a man they call Menis." Sanch opened his eyes and looked toward the rising sun, then to Lisha. He jerked his head slightly to the right and they started their search.

They moved through the hurriedly erected tents, back to where Sanch last saw Hannes. The fighting was over and even the celebration was no more. It was dawn and time for a new life for many.

A young woman ran out from between two tents and jumped onto Sanch. She threw her arms around his neck and wrapped her legs around his waist. "Thank you so very much, my lord."

Sanch supported her in his arms. "Who are you? Wait. I thought you were a child. Are you the young woman whose father was almost executed last night?"

"Yes, my lord. I am the same. I rose before the sun so I could find you, to thank you for saving my father. I am in your debt."

Lisha shook her head, her eyes rolled upward. "You *do* know he had a little help with that, don't you?" Without slowing her stride or waiting for an answer, Lisha continued on her way.

"She's right, you know. You should thank her, as well." Sanch placed his hands around the woman's tiny waist and lowered her to the ground. He pointed to Lisha, who was walking fast. "Her, over there, she had a lot to do with the rescue of you and your people."

The soft sound of little feet grew faster and louder behind Lisha, before two small arms wrapped around her waist. Lisha's body stiffened like a great tree fighting off heavy winds.

The young woman's gentle grip tightened like the perfect fit of a belt. "My lady, you fought alongside men with such grace, strength and bravery. I hope one day to fight as you do, to free slaves and protect those in need. You have shown me it is possible. Why wait to be rescued by a man, when I can raise my own sword in my defense? Thank you."

Lisha lowered her shoulders and, with a great sigh, placed her hands over those of her petite captor's. "You are welcome. I look forward to the day we will fight together to end oppression and swing our swords to vanquish any who try and stand in our way." Lisha, by now, held the woman at arms' length. She removed her hands and walked swiftly into the forest, leaving the young woman standing alone.

Sanch, also alone, said, "I guess I'll go find Menis on my own, then."

"I will join you on your search, if you will have me, my lord." The young woman had run back to Sanch. She wrapped her arm around his and matched his pace.

They were soon on the edge of the camp just outside the village where Hannes, Menis and the other men lived. The morning was still debating the night for the right to appear.

The woman said, "After a battle, they like to set up camp on the outskirts of our village to celebrate. It keeps the mess outside."

"Phew! I can see why," Sanch said. "I can smell the stench of vomit and wine."

"Other things, too," she said. "These men lie where they had their last drink, some in their own piss."

She and Sanch walked passed women and men lying together right in the open, in various stages of nakedness. They turned to each other, Sanch shook his head and laughed. "Too drunk, or too lazy, to seek shelter?"

"Perhaps, a little of both, my lord." She entwined her fingers with his and they continued their search for Menis.

Sanch stopped and pulled her close when birds suddenly flew from behind bushes.

"Sanch, Sanch!"

Still hovering over the woman, Sanch turned.

Menis ran towards them. "I am very happy you did not leave without me." The large man's voice rode a heavy breeze like a gentle feather. "Where are you two heading?"

Sanch loosened his grip on the handle of his sword and straightened up, leaving the woman hunched down before him. "We were looking for you." He reached for her hand and helped her stand. "Trust me, I was not leaving without you. I can use all the help I can get."

She folded her hands behind her back and fixed her eyes on the ground.

"I know you," Menis said. "You're that girl whose father we saved. How is the old man?" Menis arched his back and placed his hands on his knees so he could look into her eyes.

"He is fine, my lord. Happy to be alive and I have all of you to thank for my father's life." She raised her eyes to look at Menis.

"Now that you've found us, tell me where can we get some breakfast?" Sanch rubbed his stomach and pointed to the ever-rising sun. "We must leave, as soon as possible, but not without something to eat."

"I will take you both to get food." Menis rose up like a tree over them. He led them to a fire surrounded by his family and friends.

Sanch said, "The heat from this fire is like a comforting embrace from the cold of the morning."

"The food's not bad, either." Menis reached into the pot. "Oh! It's hot, too!" The big man blew on his fingers with a mouth full of food.

Those gathered laughed loudly and heaped more on a plate for the young giant.

"Well, look who it is," Hannes said. "Even Thrant has pulled himself from his tent to join in on our morning meal. Still wearing your companions like clothing, I see."

"They are more like decoration or jewelry, I think," Thrant said. "The sun is nearly level with the horizon. This is a rather late breakfast, don't you think?" He threw his arm over Sanch's shoulder. "Don't you think we should say our goodbyes and be on our way? We'll take our *lunch* with us."

Sanch nodded. "Yes, we should leave. Time waits for no man–" he turned to look for Lisha "–or woman, and all this talk of reminiscing and remembering is wasting time. We have places we must be." H looked around again. "Has anyone seen Lisha? We need her."

"I think she is hiding over there. That's where she was when I saw her." Thrant pointed towards the river.

Turning and releasing his shoulder from Thrant's grip, Sanch hurried to the riverbank. "I'll go get her. The rest of you just be ready to go. We will leave as soon as we return."

Menis ran to catch up with him. "I'm going to say goodbye to my friends and family still inside the village. They will be proud to know I am joining the son of Lackshin on his quest."

Sanch smiled. "Good, you do that, and I will be back, after I have found Lisha."

Thrant said, "Ladies, I hope to see you all, again, on my return. For now, I must prepare for a grand adventure."

Sanch headed through the woods toward the river to where Lisha was bathing. He crouched low and moved bushes that blocked his line of sight to the river. Rather than approaching her outright or calling her name, he hunkered down, transfixed.

"Are you just going to stand there and watch or are you going to jump in?" Sanch undressed and jumped in the river with her. "I knew you wanted me."

"In your dreams, boy. I just got sick of smelling you." She turned her back to him and swam to shore.

"Where are you going? I just got here!"

"I'm done, but you should take your time. You need it." She laughed and walked to a smooth area along the riverbank.

He watched her emerge from the water, naked and wet. "Well, you were right. I feel much better now. I did need a bath." He dressed on the run while he caught up to her. "I've wanted to ask you something for some time, now."

Lisha glanced at him without turning her head. "As long as you don't ask—"

"—What was your father like?"

"My father was kind and gentle. He made my mother laugh and he taught me everything I know about a sword, including how to use one."

"From what I've seen, he taught you well." His eyes dropped toward the ground. "My father died before I had a chance to learn anything from him,"

"How *did* you learn all you know?" she asked. "How did you come to be so skilled with a sword?"

"I taught myself. It took longer than if I'd had a father to teach me, but, still, I learned what I needed to know. Besides, my mother comes from a clan of women who are no strangers to the sword. What I couldn't teach myself, she was eager to show me."

Lisha stopped and smiled at him. "She and her warrior clan can be proud. You taught yourself well and I suspect much of that is natural talent."

"Thank you. I suppose I didn't have much of a choice, did I?"

They walked in silence for a while, then he said, "What was it like to have a fa—" He stopped, cupped his hand to his ear and reached for his sword. "Do you hear that?"

"I don't hear anything."

"Listen. There's something out there."

"You're imagining things. There's noth—"

Something that appeared to be half-man and half-beast jumped from a tree, no more than seven feet from where Sanch and Lisha stood, hands on swords, ready for battle. The beast stopped in front of the duo and looked at them. It walked around them, hunched over, head cocked to one side. It circled closer, sniffing the air. With a soft, mewling sound and a flash of teeth, as quickly as the man-beast had jumped from the tree, it turned and was out of sight, up another tree.

"Sanch, what *was* that?"

"I don't know, but I told you I heard something."

"Have you ever seen anything like it before?"

After a moment, Sanch said, "Yes, but that was a long time ago and it was not fully grown. I now realize I felt its presence when I was alone, before I met you."

"What was that all about?" She started walking but looked over her shoulder, into the forest. "Why did it jump out of the trees and circle us but leave us alone that way?"

"I think I may have saved its life and sent it on its way, when we were both much younger. Why do you ask?"   She shrugged. "I don't know. I was just wondering. That's all."

Sanch picked up his pace to keep up with her. "Let's go get the others. We have a long journey ahead of us."

* * *

Sanch turned to Thrant. "Tell me, how long ago was it that my father's sword was thrown into Hell's Doorway?"

"It's been eight years since I was ordered to dispose of Shallin."

Sanch turned to face the older man. "*You* were the one who did that?"

Thrant sighed. "It was my job. I had to do it or give my life."

"But, I don't understand. Why?" Sanch's fists dropped to his sides.

"Because, I saved the life of someone Sillack wanted dead."

Lisha stepped between them. "His father, the only man who can touch that sword, is dead! Why speak now? Why even take us on this fool's quest?"

"Because, now that you have freed me, I can right some of the wrongs I've committed."

"But, what good will it do, if no one but Lackshin can touch the sword? How will it help to find it?"

Sanch said, "Lisha, let him be, he's here to help us, not to be questioned by you."

"I just wish to know who or what we are dealing with. You need—I need to know."

Thrant's expression softened. "Lisha you know who I am, *what* I am. I'm your father's brother."

Sanch said, "That would make him your—"

"—That would make him *nothing* to me," Lisha growled. She spurred her horse and rode off ahead of the others. Sanch started after her but Thrant touched his shoulder. "Leave her. She just needs to be alone."

They rode at a comfortable pace, with Lisha traveling faster until Menis asked, "What is that sound?"

"What sound? I don't hear anything."
Sanch quieted his horse and dismounted. He
turned his head, straining to hear.

"Horses," Menis said.

"I agree." Sanch returned to the saddle on
Aly's back.

"Sanch! Menis! Those aren't horses,"
Thrant yelled. "They are Rinnis and by the sound
of it, they are coming this way."

"So? What do we care?" Menis shifted in
his saddle.

Thrant said, "If you care to live, you will
get Lisha and follow me."

Menis encouraged his horse into a gallop
and in moments, returned with Lisha.

Sanch asked, "What are they and why are
they after us?"

"They are dark creatures and they just
want to kill us. They aren't after us, specifically.
It's nothing personal."

"Oh, so that's supposed make us feel
better? Because it's not personal?"

Thrant yelled over his shoulder as he
rode. "Shut up, Sanch! Run before we give you to
them." He rode ahead, but stopped his horse at a
crossroad, marked an X in the sand, with his
sword. "Don't stop to watch me! Ride!"

"Why did you do that?" Sanch asked.

"Just ride! Hurry! I'll explain later."

Lisha called out, "Three are still coming. What do we do now?"

"Trust me. I know what to do. Come, now! Hurry!"

Thrant took them to another crossroad, made the same mark, but this time he led them down a side road. Lisha said. "This is such odd behavior. What's next, howling at the moon?"

"No. Now, we find a tree and climb it."

"Oh, yeah, that sounds like a great plan," she said. "I'd rather fight them."

"Be quiet. You do *not* want them to hear you." Thrant released his horse with a slap on the backside and the others did the same.

The Rinnis were getting closer.

Thrant whispered, "Hurry! Get as high as you can." He signaled with a finger over his lips for everyone's silence. In minutes, the Rinnis were below the tree where Sanch had hidden. They did not look up, but shuffled and snorted at the human footprints at the base of the trees.

Sanch almost lost his grasp on the limb he had chosen and was repositioning himself when he heard a loud snap. The Rinnis stopped and looked forward as

Sanch started to fall. The branch he'd selected had given way.

After falling a few feet, Sanch felt a large hand wrap around his wrist. The creature he and Lisha had seen earlier held him tightly and with its other hand, motioned, as Thrant had, for Sanch to remain quiet.

The Rinnis lost interest in the trees and footprints and trotted away. As soon as they were out of sight, the man-beast released its grip on Sanch's arm and he fell to the hard earth with a thud. He looked up, but the creature was nowhere to be seen. "He could've let me down easier than that."

Menis also checked the trees for some sign of Sanch's savior. "What *was* that?"

Lisha said, "That was the same creature Sanch and I met on our way back to the camp."

Thrant was the last to climb down from his tree. He walked next to Lisha. "Did it say anything to you?"

"No. It came and went the same way it did earlier," she said, "swiftly and silently." She moved closer to Sanch and offered her hand. "What do you think?"

He dismissed her help with a brush of his hand on hers. "I think it did not have to drop me so damn hard." He sat in the dust and brushed at something on his leg.

Lisha said, "I think we should get going."

Thrant said, "I think you are right. Menis let's go."

"What about Sanch?" Menis walked over to him, but didn't offer his hand. He reached under his arms and picked him up, standing Sanch on his feet.

"He can come, too," Lisha said.

"Thanks. So very kind of you to allow me to come along on my own quest."

They called their horses and only Lisha's required an extra whistle before it returned. They rode another half hour when Menis asked, "Where are we going, and how long before we get there?"

"It's not much farther. The volcano is right over that hill." Thrant pointed in the direction they were to ride.

"Is it guarded?" Sanch asked.

Thrant shrugged. "I don't know. I have been imprisoned many years, but I know that Sillack is not a trusting man, so I am sure he has a small band of men watching the volcano."

"But the sword is said to have been gone for eight years." Sanch hung his head. "Why keep it guarded all this time?"

"This is true. The sword was also said to have been made by the hands of gods," Thrant said.

"What are you saying, "Lisha asked, "that the sword cannot be destroyed?"

"It cannot be destroyed by man." Thrant's voice was even, as if he were instructing a child.

"Why hasn't someone gone after it before now?" Menis asked.

"Because, everyone knew that no one but Lackshin could touch Shallin." Thrant said.

"What are we doing here, in that case?" Menis asked.

Thrant explained with the same, even-toned voice. "We have the next best thing. We have Sanch, the son of Lackshin, the only *other* man who can release the sword from her place of rest. He was thought to be dead, until now."

"Tell me, how exactly were you able to move my father's sword, if no other man can touch her."

"We did not touch her, we made a case in which to carry Shallin to the volca—" Thrant interrupted himself and stood in his stirrups. "Look! He does have men on watch."

Menis asked, "How many?"

"I see four at the front and at least ten more in the woods, give or take a man or two. Any ideas?"

"Yes. Let's get out of here!" Lisha started to turn her horse around.

Sanch looked at her with his jaw clenched. "We cannot just leave. My father's sword is in there. I need it to kill Sillack."

She said, "Looks like one is coming this way."

They rode their horses behind some trees surrounded by high shrubbery.

"He's getting closer," Menis said.

The guard ambled toward them. One of the horses nickered and the soldier stopped inches from where they were hiding. After he looked toward the sound, he shrugged and continued walking some distance to a cluster of bushes where he followed a narrow path, dropped his trousers and squatted.

Menis sighed. Lisha straightened in her saddle from where she had leaned over to calm her horse. Sanch returned his sword to its scabbard and Thrant slipped his dagger back into its sheath.

"That was close. I thought he would see us, for sure." Menis sighed again.

"Me too," Sanch said. "I thought that was it."

"We still have a small problem. How are we going to get that sword?" Lisha turned toward the men. "Thrant, these are your people. What do you think we should do?"

"First, we should decide who is going and who is staying," Thrant said.

Menis looked at each member of the group. He was bouncing on his toes.

Sanch slid from his saddle and walked forward with Aly's reins. "Since I am the only one here who can move the sword and Thrant is the only one of us who has any idea where the sword might be, he and I will be going in." He handed the reins to Menis.

"So what do Lisha and I do out here while you and he are in the volcano?"

Thrant said, "You and Lisha will make certain all of those men are not in there with us." He rode his horse next to Aly before he dismounted and put the reins in Menis' hand.

"Just how are we supposed to do that?" Lisha dismounted and thrust her horse's reins into Menis' hand, too. She crossed her arms over her chest.

Thrant rested his hand on her shoulder. "I don't know. You're a big girl. You'll come up with something." He turned and motioned to Sanch, who started walking toward the volcano.

Lisha and Menis secured the horses before they trudged through the woods to the entrance of the volcano. She held one hand out to Menis with the finger of her other hand at her pursed lips and he hunkered down to wait. She

made a chopping motion with her hand and
Menis nodded.

Lisha jogged most of the way to the
volcano. She slowed to a walk only to even out
her breathing before she slipped around a rock
and stood with her hands on her hips a few feet
away from the guard the farthest from the
entrance.

"Hey! How did you get passed the other
guards?" one of Sillack's men asked.   She
shielded her eyes from the sun with her hands
and looked around in an exaggerated display.
"What guards? There is no one out there. I just
came to say hi. So, hi." She returned the same
way she had come.

Sillack's men started yelling. "Hey, where
are you going?"

"What do you mean there are no guards?"

"Come back here!"

"Where did you come from?"

Then, they followed her. As they came
around the last big rock, Menis greeted each of
them with a powerful swing from his ax. He
tossed each man, like an old shirt, on top of the
others.

* * *

As they entered the volcano, Sanch asked,
"Which way do we go?"

"Give me a minute." Thrant's voice quivered. "It has been a long time since I was here. I'm trying to remember the way." He took a deep breath and his voice strengthened. "That is the way we need to go." He pointed.

"Are you sure?" Sanch hesitated. "You need to be absolutely certain."

"Yes, yes. That is the way," Thrant said. "I am positive."

The passage grew hotter, the deeper they traveled in the dark cave. Even the air burned.

With a slight tremor, Sanch asked, "How do you know this is the way?"

"The volcano begins in a cave near here. See that mark on the wall, the one that looks like a large hand scratched into the stone? I remember that mark."

"If you are sure, I have little choice but to trust you. You were the last man to see my father's sword and I will retrieve it."

They walked on in silence some time before Thrant spoke. "Ah, yes. I remember. When the sword went into the volcano, it went to sleep."

"It? What it?"

"It. The dragon." Thrant said. "The sword's song put the dragon to sleep."

"Dragon? What dragon?" Sanch drew his sword. "No one said anything about a dragon."

Thrant whispered, "She's sleeping, remember? She will not even know we were here."

"But if I take Shallin, won't she wake up?"

"I guess you're onto something, there, boy. Now, why didn't I think of that?"

"Thrant, how can you be so relaxed about this, this *dragon*?"

Thrant held his hands up in a sign of surrender. "This is your quest. I'm just here to help. You came looking for me, if you recall. If you want to go back, I am more than happy to leave."

Sanch shook his head firmly. "No, that will not be happening. Not today. I have come too far to let my father down, and that I will not do!"

With his hand on the young man's shoulder, Thrant said, "I see you *are* the man your father was. This is good. Now, let's go collect your sword. Dragon be damned!"

Chapter Four

"Where did they come from?" Menis pointed toward the nearby woods.

Lisha said, "This can't be good. Those two are going into the volcano."
"But the others are running right at us." Menis motioned Lisha to follow him. Lisha looked to him and nodded.

"But the guards are everywhere," Lisha said.
"This way, come on, they won't see us in here." They ran between groups of low shrubs to a thicket of wild vines near the volcano entrance. Menis pulled down a thick armful of vines, rolled them into a large ball and sat on them.
Lisha glared at him when he patted the vines next to him. "What? Do you expect me to just sit here?"
"No, we have to find Sanch and Thrant," Menis said, "or take out those guards. First, we need to plan."

* * *

Sanch and Thrant had a lot more than two of Sillack's guards to worry about. They were facing a dragon that slept on a large island surrounded by a river of lava deep in the volcano. A faint glare came from a second much smaller island. Just a small ray of sunlight managed to make its way into this part of the cave. The thin beam reflected off an exposed part of the blade of Lackshin's sword.

Sanch becoming tired, "How much further now?"

Thrant mopped his face on his sleeve. "I don't know, but it can't be far. Her cave is in the belly of the volcano and it's getting hotter by the second." Sanch pulled him into the shadows. "Shhh," With his hand firmly covering Thrant's mouth. "Over there." It looked like her scales were glowing from some unknown light source, beautiful and asleep.

"Yes, I think that is her," Thrant whispered.

"What now, do I just take it or do I ask her for it?" Sanch asked unsure of his next move.

Thrant looked into his eyes, "That, Sanch, it's up to you, but just don't get us killed."

"Yes it is up to me. This in my father's sword and I must retrieve it."
He placed his hand on the boy shoulder. "He is gone Sanch, that is your sword you must retrieve."

Sanch stepped out from the shadows, and into the dragon den where his father's sword slept.

"I am Sanch, son of Lackshin, heir to the sword known as Shallin I have come for her."

The dragon lifted her head and looked up at Sanch. She moved slowly toward Sanch looking him over. She towered over him. Her scales still glowing a shade of green in which Sanch had never seen the likes of. It looked emerald but a shade all it's own. She turned away from Sanch and blew a ball of fire into the river of lava causing it to overflow. She then turned to Sanch with steam still bellowing from her nose. And with piercing eyes she spoke.

"I have been waiting for you, Sanch, son of Lackshin. Step into the light. Let me get a better look at you so that I can see how you have grown."

Sanch knew nothing of this beast, but she certainly knew of him.

Sanch took a step forward, "How do you

know of me dragon?"

A smirk came across the beast's face, "Your father and I are old friends."

Intrigued, Sanch asked, "You knew my father?"

The dragon replied with a sneer, "Yes, all to well."

* * *

"So what do we do?" she questioned, looking to him for a plan.

Menis, trying to stay alert to the surroundings, "I don't know Lisha, but we need to get in there to help them."

Lisha whispered, "Menis, I have an idea. Wait until they are on the other side of the camp and make a run for it."

Menis smiled then peered out from the safety of the vines. He grinned at Lisha as he picked up a fist-sized stone. He bounced the stone in his palm, letting the weight drop his hand as it hit.

That made it sound as if there were movement on the other side opposite from where they were hiding.

One of the guards quickly turned, "What was that?"

"I don't know." Replied one of the others.

That sent only some of them way. Leaving them not as many of them to attend to.

Menis turned to her, "I think this is going to be the best chance we have; we should g-."

She quickly hugged him, "Good work Menis."

And she was off. They ran unnoticed by the men until it was to late. They cut them down quickly without losing any momentum and right into the volcano in search of their friends.

"Now, which way?" Lisha asked, wanting a quick answer. He shrugged, "I don't know but I did come up with the last plan so it is your turn."

"Fine then. I think we should go this way." Lisha pointed to the cave nearest the entrance.

Menis started toward the cave, but she put her hand on his shoulder. "I changed my mind," she said. "That cave feels wrong."

"Good choice, let's go," Menis ran ahead toward the cave not wasting precious time.

They made their way quickly down the dark hole to where Sanch and Thrant were face to face with a dragon.

Lisha now sweating wiped her face with her forearm. "It's getting hot in here."

Menis, a little worried, replied, "I know, I think it's because we are going deeper into a volcano."

Lisha stopped dead in her tracks and motioned for Menis to look. He pulled close to her and bent down to her level to better see what she saw. The axes on his back scraped the wall of the cave. Lisha placed one hand on Menis as she leaned around him to see the two guards who had entered the volcano before them, picking their way around the pools of lava, easing closer to Sanch, who faced the dragon.

"So Lisha, how do you want to do this?"

Lisha looked to where the guards were headed, "I do not know but we have to do it quickly."

The two guards had already spotted Sanch and Thrant and there was little time before things got really ugly.

Sanch did not notice the two guards and continued to speak unaware he was being watched. "When did you know my father?"
The beast's voice softened, "A long time before you were born." She said. "He and I fought wars together."

The young warrior queries about the singing sword. "So why does she sing?"
He could hear the sadness in the dragon's tone, "It sings a sad song. It longs to fight for good in the hands of your father."

"But I am not him," Sanch said, as if apologizing to both the dragon and the sword.
The dragon firmly replied, "Yes, but you are of your father and your fight is the same. Is it not?"
"Yes, it is a fight for good," Sanch confirmed.
The beast nodded, "Yes, and that is the fight we long for."
As the dragon looked to Sanch's hands, "So, I see you have the sword I gave to your father to give to you."
He looked down to his sword, "This is from you?"
"Yes, I wanted you to have a great sword just as he did," she reached down and with a single claw touched the handle of his sword.
Not seeing the two guards moving closer to them Thrant looked on as Sanch and the dragon continued their convocation. Good thing Lisha and Menis made it in when they did. As the two guards closed in on Sanch and Thrant, Menis and Lisha closed in on them. One of the guards slowly drew his sword, the other guard quickly followed suit.
"Look, Lisha, they are getting ready to

attack!"

"It has to be now." Lisha with her sword already in hand replied.

After saying that, she and Menis charged the two guards.

They ran out into the open where they could be seen.

"Look out Sanch; behind you!" her voice echoed.

A startled Sanch turned, "Lisha what is going on?" as he turned around.

In the corner of his eye, he spotted the guard advancing. In one motion he swung his sword and cut the guard's head off. The guard did not notice the dragon from the direction they entered the chamber, and that cost him his life. The dragon grabbed the guard penetrating his chest with her mighty claws. With blood spurting from his mouth he screamed. The dragon threw his swaggering bleeding body into the river of lava. His body quickly burned.

"Lisha, Menis what is going on?" He ran to his friends.

Lisha, breathing heavily, "Menis and I followed those two guards in. We had to make sure they did not get the jump on you two."

Thrant reasoned with everyone. "That's nice, but I know these guards and I am sure the others are not too far behind."
And right he was, four more guards poured into the cave with more not far behind.

The dragon turned to Sanch, "I think it is time for you to get your father's sword and for you to be on your way."

"And what will come of you, won't they find you?" questioned Sanch, very worried for the beast.

She reassured him, "I'll be fine, just get the sword."

As Sanch got closer to the sword, the singing became louder. It got so loud that it was unbearable to the others in the cave. Lisha, Menis and Thrant fell to their knees, holding their ears, as did Sillack's men. The cave started to come apart. Rocks fell from the walls, but Sanch still continued walking to Shallin. As all of this went on, no one seemed to notice the dragon was glowing brighter the closer he got. As Sanch reached the sword the singing was not only a song, it was a vibration in the whole volcano.

"What is going on?" asked one of the guards who had just entered the volcano. Another guard responded, "I don't know, but the sound is coming from down there. Let's go check it out."
When Sanch finally closed his hands around the handle of Shallin, everything suddenly stopped and it was silent. By that time the cave was still too badly damaged to stay. And if that was not bad enough, the volcano became active. The river of lava that flowed around the islands began to rise.

"We have to get out of here," shouted Thrant, "this place is coming down."

"In there, in there is where I heard that sound." More men ran into the cave.

Thrant looked up at the dragon, "The rest of the guards are coming, is there any other way out of this place?"

"Yes, we have no time to fight them all before this cave comes down on all our heads." Sanch added.

The beast looked around, "Yes, Sanch, you and your friends climb onto my back, I am going to fly you out of here."

They wasted no time climbed onto her back and just as the other guards entered the cave, the dragon caught an up draft under her out stretched wings and took flight with Sanch and the others up through the mouth of the volcano. The lava quickly filled the dragon's old home killing the men left behind. The lava climbed the walls chasing them up. As they flew, Lisha lost her grip and started to slide off the dragon's back. She reached out for one of the strap's that held Menis's ax to his back. She closed her fist around nothing and she went toward the heat of the lava that closely followed them. With speed and no concern for his own safety, Thrant threw out his hand, grabbing Lisha's wrist right below her closed fist. His other hand griped onto the dragon, with blood running down his arm from the razor sharp scale cutting into his palm. He pulled her to his chest. Under her, he could see the river of lava closing in on them. She threw her other arm around her uncle's neck. Her face pressed to his.

"I have you my little Lisha."

Just as they cleared the volcano, it erupted, springing lava hundreds of feet into the air, barely missing them.

They landed safely and now out of danger, Sanch still had one more question.

He looked up at the dragon with his father's sword now in his hand where it belonged, "After all you have done for my friends and I, I still do not know what to call you."

The dragon smiled, "You can call me what your father, my friend called me; you can call me Shallin."

And in a mist she was gone from their sight.

As they all looked around in wonder Lisha reached out to touch the misty essence, it was a cold vapor. She turned to Sanch. "So what do we do now?"

Sanch with a calm in him now, "Lisha, we found Shallin, so now it is time for Sillack to know I'm coming for him."

Chapter Five

On the other side of the forest
At the same time on the other side of the forest, what seems like the other side of the world. Sillack's men were reporting to him. His chamber was a gloomy darkness. There was a window that allowed in some streams of light. On the wall there were trophies from kingdoms and villages he had destroyed in his reign of terror. There were

weapons and instruments of torture that he particularly enjoyed. There was one in particular that was his favorite; it's function was to keep the prisoner alive long enough to beg for Sillack to have mercy. As Alshin, one of Sillack's guards, entered this room he approached Sillack sitting on his blood stained throne. He told him of his confrontation with one claiming to be the son of Lackshin, and the one he had imprisoned who had escaped.

"What do you mean Thrant escaped?!" Sillack questioned angrily.

Taking a step back the guard began stumbling over his words, "Thrant was rescued by a boy claiming to be the son of Lackshin."

Slamming his fist down and in a low rumble Sillack said, "That is not possible, I had him killed."

   "Are you sure he was killed?" The guard questioned with a quiver in his voice. "They could have taken him to safety."

   "If so, he will not get away from me this time," Sillack declared. "Find him and bring him to me, I will kill him myself this time. Alshin, don't fail me, bring me back the son of Lackshin immediately."

Nervously Alshin answered, "Yes my lord, I will not fail you."

Sillack placed his hands on Alshin's shoulder, "Oh yes, bring back that traitor, Thrant, to me as well."

Alshin left Sillack's chamber in search of Sanch. Alshin wanting to move fast gathered a small force by choosing 50 of the best men in Sillack's larger army, and ordered a larger force to ready

*themselves and to join them as soon as they are
ready to move out. Alshin got his men together
and headed to the volcano where Sanch was last
seen. That alone made his chances of finding
Sanch all that better. Since Sanch was hiding in
that direction, they were going to have to run into
one another sooner or later...and then what?*
Alshin went through the countryside giving the
command to burn and pillage all of the villages in
their path. They questioned the people of the
villages, killing those who had no information to
give. Alshin wanted to make sure that Sanch did
not get past him and his men, because that could
cost them their lives.

"Alshin," shouted one of the guards, "what
should I do with this woman?"   Alshin
turned to see what woman, "Does she know of
his whereabouts?"

"No my lord, I know nothing of this man or his
whereabouts." The woman said as she fell to her
knees.

"Then kill her," replied Alshin.
The guard stumbled, "But she said she knows
nothing; do I still need to kill her?"

Alshin glared at the man. The frightened
guard then took her away and did just what he
had been ordered to do. Alshin went on looking
for Sanch and any signs that he may have passed
this way. His men tortured the men and caged
the women and still no sign of Sanch.
Unbeknown to him, Sanch was not far from the
village Alshin was now searching. He was just on
the other side of a hill near the village he and his
men were burning. One of the guards took a man
out in front of everyone in the village.

The guard proceeded in a very loud voice, "If someone knows anything of the one called Sanch, speak now and save this man's life."

One woman shouted from the crowd, "We know nothing of this man. Let him go!"

The guard snapped back," I will let him go when you tell me what you know."

"But we know nothing," the crowd pleaded.

Alshin stepped in, "I believe them."

The guard quickly asked, "Should I let him go?"

"No, kill him anyway and let's get out of here," Alshin sneered.

Not too far away, Sanch spoke, looking from the distance, "Lisha, look over there. It looks like that village is on fire, we should help."

"Sanch we should just stay out of it, we have somewhere to be." Lisha said quickly to get any silly thoughts out of his crazy head. Sanch turned to Thrant, "Thrant I'm never too busy to help those who need my help."

At the same time Menis was making his way to the hill. Menis called to Lisha, "What are you doing?" Turning to her he added, "There are people on the other side of that hill that need our help."

Sanch joined him, "He's right, let's go, time is wasting."

Sanch repeated himself, "Let's go... Thrant if you don't want to come you can stay here."

They started on their way to the village. Quickly mounting the horses and road hard to the village, and not a moment to soon. They got there just in time to see Alshin's guard about to cut off a man's head in front of a pleading crowd.

Lisha, very nervous now but wanting to help said, "What are we going to do Sanch?"

Sanch snapped back, "Lisha there is no time for a plan, follow me."

Sanch drew his father's sword, still having his sword strapped to his back. He went through Alshin's men like a hot knife through butter, and not far behind him were Lisha and Menis. Sanch made his way to the guard who was ready to cut off the head of the village man. Sanch stopped the guard with his father's sword. The guard did not see Sanch making his approach, but when he did, it was too late. Sanch took the guard's head before he could turn to see the young warrior sword. At that time, Lisha and Menis were at his side with their swords and ax in hand ready for a move to be made. The village people were running to safety, they were saved from Alshin and his men. The small army of guards gathered together as if ready for another assault on Sanch, Lisha, and Menis. Out from the army of guards came Alshin with sword in hand.

"So we meet once more, son of Lackshin," Alshin yelled to his men. Sanch started to approach him, "Yes, it's been to long. Have you missed me?"

Angered by Sanch's mocking, Alshin responded, "It has been a long time, but why has it taken you so long to find me? How many village people did I have to kill for you to come?"

Sanch's blood started to boil, "Well I'm here now, what do you have in mind?"

"The last time we met you got lucky," Alshin snickered, "your girlfriend saved you and got you away from me."

Outraged, Sanch replied, "She is not my girlfriend, and she did not need to get me away from you."

Alshin laughed, "Well prove it, and fight me."

Sanch advanced, "It would be my pleasure!"

Sanch stuck his father's sword into the ground and pulled his sword out. Sanch and Alshin engaged in battle. Alshin swung his sword with evil in his eyes. Sanch ducked out of the way of Alshin's swing and kicked him in the back, knocking him off his feet.

Alshin rising to his feet proclaimed, "That was good—for someone with no real training."

With confidence in his voice Sanch exclaimed, "I don't need training to beat you, I have something you don't have."

"And, son of Lackshin, what is that?" Alshin retorted. With a smirk, Sanch replied, "That would be skills and I have a lot of that."

Alshin shouted, "Sanch, shut up and fight!" He came at Sanch like a stampeding buffalo. Sanch held his ground. Alshin lunged his sword at Sanch. Sanch put up his sword just in time to block Alshin's sword. Slipping off to one side, giving him the opportunity to attack his head, but instead he cut his face.

"First blood!" shouted Sanch.

"What have you done? You cut me," Alshin said in shock.

"Yes I did, did I not," gloated Sanch. "Well, I could have killed you, but I'll save that for later."

"Later? There will be no later, not for you, I'm going to kill you now," Alshin declared.

At that time, Alshin raised his sword and started his charge on Sanch. He ran roaring at Sanch. Sanch gripped his sword, tilted it, and stood ready. Alshin came down hard. Stumbling, Sanch knocked him off his balance. He continued his attack on Sanch until he had his back to a tree.

"Now Sanch, it's your turn to bleed, and I'll be the one doing the cutting."

Sanch looked at him and smiled which made him mad. Alshin swung for Sanch's head. Off to the side there was a scream. It was Lisha. Sanch planted his feet, ducked, and allowed Alshin to cut the tree almost in half. That allowed Sanch to then cut a lock of his hair. Sanch then turned to him. "And on that note, my friends and I will be taking our leave now."

Sanch then put his sword away, grabbed Shallin, stepped back and raised Shallin to his chest and bowed while extending his arms outward.

"I'll be seeing you, Alshin," with a glimmer in his eyes accompanied with a smirk. "Oh yes, tell Sillack I'll be seeing him also."

"Guards, get them!" shouted Alshin with his sword still buried in the tree, "don't let them get away!"

Sanch, Lisha and Menis exited just as they entered, as they fought for their lives, sword to sword and hand to hand. The three warriors made their way from Alshin and his men.

Back in hiding, Thrant waited nervously for Sanch and the others. "I did not think I was going to see you three again," Thrant sighed.

Lisha smirked, "Thank you Thrant, but we

did fine without your help."

Sanch laughed, "Lisha said it; we did not need your help after all."

"Menis, look over that hill and see if they are still coming," Sanch asked.

With slight hesitation, Menis answered, "No Sanch, they are no longer coming, but they are getting on their horses heading off in the other direction."

"They are going back to Sillack and we should follow them. They will take us to him."

Sanch commanded the others, "Get your things together and get ready to move out."

Menis turned to Thrant, "Are you coming this time?"

"Yes Menis, I will be coming this time," Thrant nodded.

Lisha gave at a little laugh, "Well that's good of you, you know we just can't do this without you." Sanch did not want to waste any time responding, "Are you all done, can we go now?"

"Sanch, I'm ready to go on," Menis quickly jumped to his side.

Sanch smiled, "Thank you Menis, let's go."

Lisha with hands on her hips, "Oh don't worry Sanch I'm coming too."

Smiling to himself, "Oh thank you Lisha, you know you are welcome to join us anytime."

Sanch quickly added, "Let's go, they're moving out and we need to keep up with them."

Thrant slightly hesitant said, "Are you sure they are going back to Sillack?"

Turning around, "What do you mean Thrant? Why would they not be going back to

Sillack?"

He explained, "Alshin is on a mission, and that mission is to bring you, son of Lackshin, back to Sillack."

"So what do you think their next move is going to be?" Sanch asked, not knowing what to do now.

Thrant thought for a moment, "They might head to another village and start their killing again."

"So then I guess we should stay close to them and make sure that does not happen," Sanch replied.

Sanch, Lisha, Menis, and Thrant started after Alshin and his men making sure to keep a safe distance. They rode straight for days trying to keep up. They only stopped to sleep and eat when Alshin and his men stopped, and that was not often enough. They rode long and hard as if the lives of people they did not even know depended on it. Sanch and his companions stayed on their heels. They were able to stay out of sight because if they were to be seen, they would have a fight on their hands. Sanch did not speak much, staying locked in on Alshin and what they were up to. Sanch observed, "Look, they are stopping and regrouping on Alshin."

"What are they doing Sanch?" Lisha questioned.

"I don't know Lisha, it looks like they are making some kind of plan."

Menis keyed in, "They must be, look, they are changing their course."

"Yes." Sanch agreed, "Menis you're right they are changing course, but where are they going now.

Thrant do you have any idea where they might be going?"

"Yes Sanch, by their course change they are heading away to a small town not too far from here." Very confused Sanch asked him, "But why would they make that change to that town?"
Thrant looked at Lisha, "They're trying to lure us out of hiding."
Menis with his eyebrows raised, "How would going to this town do that?"
Thrant lowered his head, "That is not just any town, that is the town of my people."
"They are not just your people, Thrant, they are my people as well," Lisha glared at Thrant.
Sanch realizing this was personal asked, "Is there a faster way to get to your town, that would get us there before Alshin?"
Thrant took a moment to think, "Yes, there is a faster way but it is a lot harder then the way they will be taking."
Menis agreed with Sanch, "If that is what it's going to take, then let us be on our way, time is wasting."
They mounted up and rode long and hard, Thrant was right, this was a much more difficult path to take, but they had little choice if they planned on getting there before Alshin. They stayed one step ahead, but they did not know what their plans were. What were they going to do once they got there, and were we going to be able to stop them? Those were the type of things Sanch was forced to ask himself.
Sanch blurted out, "Thrant, are you sure that you know where you are taking us?"

Annoyed by this questioned, Thrant answered, "Yes, I am sure, I can get to my own town."

Menis chimed in, "But are we going to be there before Alshin and his men is what's important?"

Thrant told them, "We will get there at least a day before them."

"That is good time, and would give us time to come up with a plan," said Menis.

Sanch looked over to Lisha, "Are you okay, is everything alright?"

She said in a low voice, "I'm fine, I just want to get there before they do."

"Lisha, we all want to get there before they do," said Sanch.

All this time, they were steadily moving through, not missing a beat.

"I think we need to stop and get some rest and something to eat," Thrant suggested.

"No, we need to move on," said Lisha disagreeing with her uncle.

Sanch put his hand on her shoulder. "No, he is right, we need to keep our strength up. If we get there and we can't fight then what good are we to the people of the town? Your people Lisha." She was calmed a little by his touch, "Okay, fine," a frustrated Lisha replied, "let's eat, but make it quick."   "Yes Lisha, we will make it quick," assured Menis.

"Yes quick," confirmed Sanch.

They sat down and had a quick meal, then were on their way to the town. Even with their stop to eat they were still going to be at least a day ahead of Alshin and his men. They stayed fast and steady on their way.

"Lisha, why is it that you and Thrant do not act more like family?" Sanch wondered, "Your family and you should get along."

"We don't, so just drop it," Lisha snapped at Sanch.

"Thrant, why does she hate you?" A still curious Sanch inquired, "Was it something you did in your past life in service of Sillack?" Thrant shrugged his shoulders, "I could not answer that. She has never told me what it was that I did."

"Shhh, keep it down, I hear something," said Menis quietly as he waved his hand in a downward motion. "It's coming from over there," He pointed.

"What is it?" Sanch whispered.

Menis whispered, "I don't know—look!"

"Sanch, it's the creature that saved you from falling out of that tree," said Thrant.

Sanch was amazed, "Is that thing following us, and if it is why?" Lisha asked as she looked at Sanch," If you really want to know so bad go and ask it."

"Are you crazy?" Sanch replied, "Do you see the size of that thing?"

Lisha snickered, "Why are you worrying about that thing? It saved your life; do you think it is going to kill you now?"

Sanch gave her a glare, "No, I think it might eat me."

Just as he said that, it looked up at Sanch as if it heard him, then ran off into the woods. Menis looked at Sanch, "What was that all about Sanch?"

"I don't know, Menis, that was strange."

"Oh well, let's move on, we are wasting time,"
Lisha said.

Before Sanch could agree with her a wild boar
from out of nowhere charged at Sanch. He went
for his sword, but it would have been too late.

"Sanch!" shouted Lisha, "look out."

Just as she said that, the strange creature
following Sanch leaped out of nowhere to his
rescue again. It grabbed the boar, broke its neck,
and threw it clear off of Sanch.

"Well, thank you, once again," said Sanch.
It looked back at Sanch and ran off once more.
Menis shook his head, "That thing is strange, and
it seems to be all about keeping you safe."

"That does seem to be true Menis, let's go,
time is wasting," Sanch said bitterly.

Sanch and the others continued on their
way. They remained days ahead of Alshin and
his men.

"How much further until we reach your
village?" Sanch asked Thrant.

"Not much further, just over that next
hill."

Lisha looked at Sanch. "Do you have a
plan for when we get there?"

Sanch shook his head, "Lisha, I have no
idea what I am going to do. If anyone has an idea
now is a good time as any to say something."

Thrant spoke, "I think we should wait until
we get there to decide what we need to do."

"I agree," said Sanch, "that I think is the
best way to approach this fight."

"Look," shouted Menis, "is that what I
think it is?"

"Yes, that is Alshin and his men. It looks

like they are at least two to three days away from
the village," said Thrant.

"Come on let us go," said Sanch, "I want to
be in that village before night fall."

After saying that, Sanch started on his way
to the village. Not far behind came Lisha, Menis,
and Thrant.

Chapter Six

With speed and determination they rode like
the devil himself was in pursuit of them. They
would stop only to eat, and no longer than
needed.

"Thrant, are we close?" Menis asked again.

"Just over that ridge. Lets at least make that
ridge, then we can get rested and get started on
the defense," Thrant suggested.

"That sounds good to me," said Menis, "as long as
we get some rest before we go."

Sanch could finally see it, "Is that it, is that your
village?"

"Yes Sanch, that is my home."

Lisha quickly added, "Don't you mean our
home, Thrant?"

"Yes Lisha, I meant to say our home. I did not mean to leave you out," Thrant smiled at her. Sanch reminded the two, "We are here to do one thing and that is to protect your people and their home. So can you both try to get along? It's going to be important for them to see you two ready to fight together."

Lisha and Thrant looked at each other then looked at Sanch and nodded. "That's good," said Sanch, "I'm glad we can all get along."

After saying that, Lisha and Thrant both rode off and went their own way.

"Hey, where are you going? We have a village to save," Sanch shouted.

Sanch then went after them with Menis not too far behind.

After catching up with Lisha and Thrant they made their way back to camp for some well-needed rest, and something to eat. Not spending much time resting they were soon on their way to the village. They knew who Thrant was right away, but Lisha they did not recognize. She was just a child when she and her father left the village.

"Lisha, why is it that no one knows who you are?" Menis questioned.

"Because Menis, they do not know me as I am now," she tried to explain.

"What do you mean?" asked Menis. She continued, "I was just a little girl when my father and I left this place."

"Why did you and your father leave?"

A somber look takes over her face. "After my mother died, my father no longer wanted to stay here. There was too much here to remind him of her, and he loved her too much to be around so much pain. So he took me and our things and we left."

Menis felt horrible, "Lisha, I am sorry, I did not know."

"How could you have known Menis, It is fine. I am fine."

"Lisha!" shouted Thrant, "Come over here and meet your family."

"Is that Lisha?" asked a woman in the crowd.

"Yes it is," Thrant replied with his head up and his chest out, "that beautiful woman is Lisha, my brother's daughter and his pride and joy."

"She looks just like her mother," said the woman.

Lisha slowly made her way over to the crowd dragging her feet like a little girl on her first day of school. Thrant reached out his hand to her, and for the first time Lisha saw how proud he was of her, a girl who spent her life hating this man for something she needed to blame on someone. And it just happened to be him. Lisha reached out and took his hand. On looking was Sanch with a smile on his face. Sanch turned to Menis.

"That is more like it, we can now begin."

Sanch walked to a part of the village where there was a river. He sat down on a rock just on the shore. He was not at rest; he had a lot on his mind.

"Father, am I doing the right thing?" he said aloud. " I have managed to put the lives of peaceful people in danger, and for what, so that I can have revenge to fill the empty hole in myself? Father, this is something I should be doing alone, and not here putting these people's lives in danger. Father help me; help me keep these people alive and unharmed. Please father, don't let me let these people down, I beg of you."

Sanch leaned over the river to wash his face. He saw a reflection of a man with his hand on his shoulder. He jumped around to see who it was, but no one was there. He looked again only to see the same thing, a man with his hand on his shoulder.

"Who are you?" Sanch asked the face looking back at him.

"You have grown my son." The voice replied.

"Did you just call me son?" Sanch asked in disbelief as a cold chill ran down his back.

"Yes I did, Sanch, did you not want to speak to me?"

"Yes," Sanch replied as the words quivered from his lips, "but you are dead, you've been dead for a long time. How do you speak to me now?"

"Son, there is nothing on this earth that can keep me from you, not even death. So son what is troubling you?"

"Father, I need to know that I'm doing the right thing."

"Sanch, what is it that you feel you are doing wrong?"

"I'm putting innocent lives in danger, they could all be killed," Sanch explained.

"Son, what kind of chance would they have without you?"

"I don't know," Sanch whispered.

His father urged, "Listen, Alshin would come for these people even if you were not here. You and your friends are the only ones who might keep these people alive. These people have a chance now thanks to you."

"So, you think I'm doing the right thing?"

"I don't know about the right thing son, but you are doing what is right."

When Sanch turned to see his father, he was gone. But in the distance he did see a familiar face. It was the creature that had saved his life more than once. It stood at least 7 ft. tall and covered with pelt. It looked as if it could take on Alshin and his whole army, despite his kind and gentle face.

As Sanch tried to approach it, out of the bushes came Lisha and Menis. "You two have great timing as always. Is there something I can help you with?" Sanch sighed, "and it better be good."

"Sanch, do you think we would bother to come find you for something small?" Lisha asked.

"I guess not Lisha, so let me hear it."

"The villagers are wanting to know what we are going to do next. Thrant has informed them of the appending danger approaching."

"Lisha, Menis, is everything in place like I asked?"

"Yes we remembered all you said needed to get done as soon as we got here. It took some doing, but everything is almost finished. The villagers worked hard to get it all done the way you wanted," Lisha said with smirk.

Sanch, pleased. "Well then you can go back and tell them that we are going to fight and win, and there will be no talk of any other outcome. Has anyone checked to see where Alshin and his men are?"

Menis quickly answered, "They are still at least a day away, give or take."

"Thanks Menis. That gives us all the time we need."

"Lisha, Menis, look at that; is that not the most beautiful thing you have ever seen?" Sanch pointed.

There stood Sanch, Lisha, and Menis looking out over a lake with the dawning sun glistening off the ripples. Menis standing almost 7 ft. tall, built like an ox, with arms the size of tree trunks and Lisha, stood silently, with her long hair blowing in the wind. Sanch with his brown skin and toughened body stood barely 5 ft. 8 in. He was not a big man, yet there was something about him that worried his enemies. There was also something about him that Lisha found intriguing. Together these three were a force to be reckoned with--some would say almost unstoppable.

Off to the side stood Sanch's hairy friend looking over him like always. Sanch felt like he was being watched, a feeling he had been having since he started his quest from his home. At least he knew the eyes that were perusing him were the eyes of a friend.

"Sanch, Sanch, hurry! There's something you need to hear, quickly come on," Thrant yelled.

Sanch looked at his two friends, "Let's go. It sounds like we are needed."

Sanch, Lisha, and Menis ran back to the village.

As quickly as they could, several things that could have gone wrong were rushing through Sanch's mind: *Could Alshin have arrived already... if so, am I too late to save the people of the village?*

Sanch, growing more worried spoke aloud, "I hope not, I must hurry."

"Lisha, Menis, come on! We must hurry," Sanch said, clearly with a sound of fear in his voice. "There's no telling what could be happening to the people of the village."

Lisha tried to reassure him, "Sanch I'm sure everything is alright, Thrant just might have things to tell us."

Sanch said sternly, "You might be right Lisha, but when we get to the village I want us all to be ready to attack whatever might be in that village waiting for us."

As the team of three approached the village, they all stood ready with weapons in hand and determination in their eyes: Sanch, with sword in hand; Lisha, her sword ready and Menis, holding his mighty ax in hand, all ready to bring down anyone or anything standing in their way. As they entered the village, there stood Thrant and a woman who looked like she had much to say.

Sanch confused, asked, "Thrant, what is going here? You told us that we needed to hurry back to the village."

"Yes Sanch, I want you to meet Lisha's cousin Bethany, our best scout. She just got back with news of Alshin's present location and he is really close. We only have a day at the most until Alshin and his men arrive at the village."

"Bethany, did you happen to see how many men Alshin has riding with him?" Sanch asked gathering his breath.

Bethany sounding confidant responded, "From what I've seen he has at least 500 or so men with him. Sanch, it's nothing that we cannot handle."

"How were you able to see this; how close did you get to them?" Sanch questioned.

"I was far enough away; there was no way they would have seen me," Bethany assured the group. Sanch, quite confused by her story, commented, "How is it that you could get close enough to see that he had 500 men with him and get back here in time for dinner and say they still have a day before getting here?"

Bethany, with an impish smile on her face replied, "I knew a short cut."

Lisha and Menis trying not to laugh, holstered their weapons, and looked away from Sanch. Thrant stayed not knowing what to do or say to break the tension that was now building between Sanch and Bethany.

Sanch still not believing her story said, "And who showed you these short cuts?"

She smiled, "My father taught me how to track wild animals without being seen or heard as well. Is there more you would like to know?"

"And who is your father if I might ask?"

"That would have to be me," said an enormous man. He stood tall, shoulders like mountainsides, and hands large enough to hold cannonballs. He walked towards Sanch like a moving landmass, almost like a glacier. It was as though he was standing between Sanch and the sun.

"And who is this that is asking for me?" the gigantic man questioned. "Thrant, is this the boy you were telling me about? I was thinking he would be taller?"

Just then he looked over and to his surprise there was Lisha, a face he had not seen for years. He loved her beauty and had missed her for so long.

"Is this Lisha, my sister's child? She is beautiful. She looks just like her mother."

"My mother?" said Lisha, with a look of inquiry in her eyes.

He leaned his head back and laughter raged from this giant of a man. "You even sound like her." Sanch and Menis stepped back as if pushed by this man's voice. Lisha stepped up to this man and looked to him with a familiar face. She knew this laugh. It was a laugh she had heard before, but knew not how this could be so. He reached down and with no effort picked Lisha from the ground. He pulled Lisha to him, embracing her.

"I am your mother's brother, we, Lisha-- you and I, are family," he said gleefully.

"Come, we have so much to catch up on. I want to show you some of your mother's things."

He smiled, "Thrant, you go ahead and give the little guy anything he may need. Come, Lisha, we are going this way."

Lisha and the gentle giant slowly walked out of sight. Bethany stood there with a large smile on her face. Her lips pressed tightly together, trying to hold in her laughter. Menis, not sharing the same tact could not help but to let it all out. He was laughing so hard he had to excuse himself. Thrant had no problem keeping a straight face. He had things that were more pressing on his mind, like the safety of his people. Bethany decided her work there was done and it was time for her to be going; besides it looked like it might get a little ugly.

She spoke up, "Guys, I think I'll be leaving now."

"If I could speak with you for a moment Bethany?" said Sanch, "I would like to thank you for going out to see how much time we have before Alshin and his men get here. I would just much rather you not put yourself in anymore danger. I would just rather you stay where it's safe, that is all."

"Sanch, thanks for your concern, but I know these hills better than anyone. Anyway, I think it is time for dinner. I made it back just in time," she said sarcastically as she turned and made her way home.

As she walked away, Sanch thought to himself, *"What is it about the women of this village, beautiful, but yet hard to talk to."*

Bethany walked away, her hair a shade of red but only when the sun hits it just right. It reached midway down her back when she let it down. Before that she had it wrapped tight for her scouting trip, sure to keep it out of her way. She did not carry a sword--she had but a staff and a crossbow, two humble weapons.

She seemed to be an enigma all her own, Sanch wondered, *what is her story?*

Menis also noticed the beauty that had just stood before him.

Sanch shook his head, "Menis if you are done can you come over here with the rest of us."

"I am sorry Sanch, I forgot myself. Forgive me."

"No problem, we can't all be the size of a hillside. Besides, we have many more important things to do, but we will speak of what amuses you at a time more suiting."

"Sanch, what exactly do you have in mind for us to do."

"We should do something, we cannot just sit and wait for Alshin and his men to get here and destroy this village and its people! I will not have the blood of these people on my hands, not one!" said Sanch, passionately with the sound of anger in his words.

"Are you suggesting we go after Alshin and his men before they arrive here?" Thrant asked.

"Thrant, did you not say Bethany knew these hills better than anyone here?"

"Yes, I did say that she knows the hills better than anyone. Why, do you want her to take us to Alshin?" Thrant wondered.

"Thrant, I could not want anything less. I am not going to take Bethany anywhere she might be put in danger."

"So how did you figure we would get there without her? Not that I feel that she should go with us anyway," Menis said clearly to Sanch.

"I thought she might just be able to tell us how we could get there."

"Thrant, can you not ask Bethany to help us by telling us how to get there?" Sanch hoped. "We only have six hours until night fall. Darkness will be our best cover and put things more in our favor. If we do this right they won't know what hit them."

"I will go now and find both Lisha and Bethany to tell them of your plan," said Thrant, sounding confident of Sanch's plan.

Thrant then took his leave and went to find the girl who should be in the home of Ralyn, head of the village.

Chapter Seven

Thrant walked through the village seeing things he had not seen for ages. There was the well that his brother had pulled him from when they were just boys. And there was the log--old, broken, and rotten.

"Time has not been good to you old friend," Thrant whispered to himself as he ran his hand over the fragile bark.

He walked on, making his way to the church; he had an old friend to see. There he saw the graves of several he left behind and some he himself helped bury. He stopped and paused for a long time. This grave he stood in front of was a modest one, unlike any of the others. It had something different about it.

With a nervous tone in his voice; looking away from the grave almost as if someone was looking back at him. He built up the courage to speak. "Vaness, it has been a long time, *too* long." With tears forming in his eyes. Thrant, a man of strength, and said to have a heart of stone, began to weep as he knelt at the foot of this grave. Not being able to contain it any longer, the mass of emotions building in his chest. He had to let it all out, it was just too much to hold in for one man, no matter how strong.

"I so wish you were here to see the woman that your Lisha has become. Every time I lay eyes on her, I think how she looks so like you. Her beauty is that of a goddess, her hand strong and embracing a sword makes her a force to be respected. You see, she has taken the best of you and her father. My sister you would be proud." His eyes filled; he buried his face in his hands. Weaken from his talk with Lisha's mother Thrant struggled back to his feet.

"Are you okay Thrant?" a voice coming from behind asked.

He composed himself and turned to see who it was. It was a familiar voice and he found it to be a familiar face as well. It was Bethany coming back to look for Thrant and the others.

"I'm fine; thank you. What are you doing back here, I thought you were going home?" he said, making his way over to her.

"As I was making my way home I thought how rude it was of me not to have asked you and the others to eat with us."

"Well I'm sure, like me, they will love your family."

"Thrant, don't you mean *our* family?" Correcting him as she wrapped her arms around his waist.

"Yes, you are right, *our* family. Lets go,

we can come back and get the boys later. I have something I need to tell you."

She rolled her eyes, "Let me guess, the one you call Sanch has an idea. Am I going to like this?"

"Just hear me out, then you can tell me how much you don't like it, okay?"

As they made their way to Bethany's home, Thrant passed several new sites. There were things there that he had never seen before. There were also new faces and people he had yet to meet.

****

"This is beautiful," Lisha said in amazement.

"That is what your mother wore when she and your father were married to become one. Your mother was so beautiful; I could not believe my eyes. My sister was a woman. A beautiful one with the whole world in her future, and best of all my best friend, the one I trusted most in the world, was going to give it all to her," Ralyn said loudly, with pain that clearly showed on his face.

"Tell me what happened to my mother? I've asked my father but he tells me nothing. I stopped asking. I figured the pain of it was too much and he chose not to give me the same pain to bear." Lisha said, understandingly.

"Your father and I felt with the both of us in your mother's life that no harm could come to her. With your father, his brother and myself, we felt we were unstoppable, we always had been. Then one day, about a year after you were born, bandits unexpectedly attacked the village. Your mother being the warrior that she was fought alongside Thrant to protect the children and those who could not fight for themselves. In the fight she and Thrant were separated. Your mother, like you, was a warrior and could take care of herself. This was her crossbow that she used with the most accuracy that I have ever seen."

Ralyn handed the crossbow to Lisha. It fit her hands like it had been made for her. It felt to her like a lost relic that was meant for her to have found.

"This time, there were too many for her to handle all by herself. When Thrant had realized that they had been separated, he began to fight his way in her direction, killing everything in sight. By the time he got to her it was too late, they found the only way to stop her was to kill her. Your Thrant had to see the whole thing moments away from her. It transformed him into something, someone the people of this village said they had never seen before. When your father and I returned to the village we found Thrant on his knees covered in blood holding Vaness. Every bandit had been killed and the man who killed your mother was fully dismembered. Out of all of the bodies, his was the hardest to find. It was like Thrant had torn him apart with his bare hands."

Lisha, standing there not knowing what to say, just stared off into nothingness. It was like she could not believe what she had just heard. All this time she felt it was something else. She so wanted someone to blame.

"I have treated them so badly," she said with remorse in her voice.

"Who have you treated badly?" asked Ralyn.

The whole time she had not noticed that both Bethany and Thrant were standing in the doorway.

"Her father and I." The sound of her uncle's voice caressed the back of her neck.

"I felt the reason you two did not tell me was because you failed my mother."

"We both agreed that we had to live with the pain and there was no reason you should have to share the same pain. We never thought you would blame us for it. We both love you with all our being; you were all we had left of her. We were both willing to do whatever it took to keep you from hearing that story. So we let you go on believing what you chose to believe." Lisha looked at Thrant. "I am so..."

"It need not be said, love was the reason." Thrant said cutting her off.

"I think you two have a lot of time to make up for," Ralyn suggested to the two.

"Yes we do, but there is no time for that now. We have a lot of work to do to get ready for Alshin and his men," Thrant said, making it very clear to the others. "Plus we have all the time in the world to start being a family again."

"What was that plan that you said Sanch came up with?" Bethany asked Thrant.

"It is almost time to eat so why don't we just go get the boys and have them tell us of the plan. Besides, I want to make sure that little one, Sanch, gets something to eat," Thrant said, sounding concerned.

"We can all go so Mom can have time to get everything prepared for dinner."

"Good idea; that way we won't be in her way. Let us go and hurry back," the women quickly added.

"I have a better idea. Thrant and I will go get the boys and you two can stay and help."

"You know, Ralyn, that is a good idea. Besides, we have things we need to speak about, and you two girls can get to know one another better. Ralyn, let us go." Thrant said with a smirk.

The two of them started on their way to the front of the village where Sanch and Menis were working on a plan to better protect the village and its walls. They were looking for ways to keep Alshin and his men from entering, and if they were to get in, it would be after an abundant of casualties making his forces manageable for the small group. Sanch figured with himself, Lisha, Menis, Thrant, and those of the village who could and chose to fight, they would have a chance against Alshin and his men to defend the village and their people. The main object of defense is a 20-30 ft. high gate weighing at least 600 lbs. of dead weight. It was attached to the rest of the gate with four iron hinges to insure its strength. On the end of the gate, most distant from the hinges, was a wheel to make the gate moveable. It still took three of the villages' largest men to do so. To hold this gate in place, when closed, were large iron latches. One was attached to the moving part of the gate that dropped deep into the ground, making it sturdy, planted in its place. The second latch slid from the stationary side of the gate locking the two firmly in place.

Even with this kind of protection, Sanch and Menis still wanted something more. Menis was working on lookout towers to better survey the hills outside. The hills were covered with trees that seemed to always be in bloom. Off to the right of the village, was the valley. There was a lake where Sanch went to be alone sometimes. From the lake, one had a perfect view of the village. The village itself was built on a hill to better defend against incoming threats. The view overlooking the valley was also a plus on the location of the village. He wanted to make sure that when Alshin and his men arrived, that they would be well aware of their coming. Menis, being of a warrior clan, had new tactics that would very much help them in their fight against Alshin's men. They both knew they had to hurry, it was getting late. It was already noon and they had much to do. Sanch still had his mind set on going after Alshin and his men. Sanch by himself was seeing how fast the gate would be able to be closed at a moments notice. With all these things going on neither of them noticed Thrant and Ralyn approaching.

"Ralyn, did you do something to the gate?" Thrant asked.

"The gate is the same as it has always been, Thrant, why do you ask?"

"Look!"

Thrant pointed to this 30 ft. 600 lb. gate. A gate that normally required three large men to slam shut, Sanch was closing with little to no effort at all. Ralyn could not believe what he was seeing. This just was something that could not be possible, that gate was built to keep out armies and hundreds of men and here he looked on as a young boy barely 150 lb. easily moved it.

"Thrant, where did you find this boy?" Ralyn asked, still in astonishment.

Just as Ralyn asked the question, Menis walked by with two logs tucked under his arms.

"Why does Menis have two trees under his arms? Thrant, where did you say you found these guys?"

"Ralyn, that's the thing, I did not find them--they found me. They rescued me from Sillack's men to help them find his father's sword."

"How would you have known where the sword was?" questioned Ralyn.

"I, at one time, was one of Sillack's men, that was before he was known as Sillack. Alshin's job at one time was my job, until he became someone, something, I did not know. He went from someone who fought for a purpose to a man who wanted nothing but power. Sillack even betrayed his best friend and that is what brings these two to your village."

By that time Sanch noticed Thrant and Ralyn just standing there looking on as they fixed up and prepared the village for Alshin's and his men to arrive. Sanch ran over to greet the two warriors.

"Hey, are you two here to help?" Sanch asked curiously.

"No, Sanch," Ralyn replied, "We just came to call you boys for dinner."

"So, where are the girls?" asked Sanch.

"Who do you think is preparing dinner?" Thrant said with a snicker.

"Menis," Sanch yelled, "guess who's making dinner, man you will never guess." Menis heard Sanch yelling at him and hurried over to see what was going on. He was not sure what he had heard, but he did know he heard someone saying something about dinner and that meant food. Menis was a big guy and his stomach had been telling him it was time to eat for a while. Walking around with trees under your arms can build up a hell of an appetite, and that he had.

"Did someone say something about dinner? If not, someone is playing with my heart as well as my stomach," Menis laughed.

"Well, I have good news and bad news. The good news is dinner is ready, the bad news is Lisha and Bethany are helping with dinner," Sanch said with a smile.

"Menis, where are you going? Dinner is ready and you are going the wrong way. The house is this way," Thrant yelled out.

"I'm going to kill something to eat," Menis said, walking away.

"Come on, Menis, it's fine. My wife made all the food and the girls are just helping her get the table ready. Menis, do you really think I would let those two desecrate my wife's food, come on now."

Menis not convinced, said, "I hope you three are telling the truth. How would I face my father and his men if I die of food poisoning? Sanch, if this food kills me you can stab me with that fancy sword of yours. That way my father won't have to," he said as he made his way back to the group.

"Whatever you say, Menis, what are friends for?"

Once Menis decided to join them again, the warriors made their way back to Ralyn's home for dinner.

A dinner Menis prayed did not kill him, but a man of Menis' size need not worry himself with food poisoning, it would take far more than that to kill him. As they walked they joked of how Lisha would use her sword to cut the vegetables. And how Bethany would take her crossbow and chase the livestock around the yard, trying to kill it. And they joked about who would get the piece with the arrowhead still in it. Ralyn went on to tell them of times when Bethany took time out of her training to spend burning down the kitchen. With all of this going on, Sanch was still able to let his mind wonder to things that had been burning away at him for who knows how long. As they continued on their way, to what Menis thinks might be his last dinner, Sanch became more and more curious. There were questions Sanch had that he felt Thrant or Ralyn might have the answer to. He always wondered where Sillack came from and why had he wanted his father dead. His mother never went into detail of what happened that day; she just always said my father died saving the people of the village. Most of all, he did so to assure Sanch a brighter future. There was a break between the jokes so Sanch saw that as the opportunity to ask his questions. Not sure how they would see such a question, Sanch did what he did best.

Without missing a beat he asked, "Does anyone know why Sillack wanted to kill my father?" Sanch said in a manner as if he were just asking for the time.

Not knowing just how to answer that question, Thrant felt he was better equipped to answer these questions—and that he did.

"So Sanch, does your mother still make her famous sweet bread?" Thrant asked from memory.

"You knew my mother?" Sanch asked sounding just a little confused upon hearing that.

"Mostly by reputation. Your father spoke highly of your mother and her sweet bread. There was nothing he spoke of more then your mother. After you were born I thought he would never stop speaking of you. His boy Sanch, the way he spoke of his son and from what I see in front of me, there is only one thing I can say. You are indeed the son of Lackshin."

"But how do you know all of this Thrant?"

"Your father and I fought together to defend his kingdom from the Xyles, creatures bent on destruction of everything they came across. We are still not sure where they came from or even what they are, but all we did know was that they were ugly and fierce. Their heads where like that of rabid dogs. Hunched over they stood an average of 8 ft. tall. They had six-inch fangs and eight-inch claws. What we found to be strange was their eyes glowed green of which we have never seen before. That glow indeed worked to our advantage. There were times at night when we could look out and see the hillside covered

with a green glow," said Thrant, trying to
continue.

"What does any of this have to do with
Sillack and the death of my father?" the
frustrated Sanch asked.
"Just listen, it will all soon make sense to
you. Now tell me, do you remember a close
friend of your fathers?" Thrant asked, wondering
if that were possible.
"Thrant, I was just a small boy when my
father was killed. I can't say I remember much
before that at all."
Thrant sighed, "Well, your father had a
friend he grew up with and people came to think
them to be brothers. We called him Sill and your
father and he were inseparable. They fought
side by side and they were something to see
when they fought together. As the war ragged
on, their views began to change. Your father was
still just fighting to protect the people of his
kingdom, but Sill began to enjoy the killing and
your father saw this."
"On a day when we felt nothing could go
wrong...it did. We stopped at a river not too far
from where you found me. It was one of the
most serene places I have ever been. The water
was the clearest, you could see all the way to the
bottom. The wind was blowing in from the north,
bringing the smell of spring. I think all the
distractions of our surroundings is what made us
vulnerable. If it were not for your father and
how he always stood ready, and telling us all to
do the same, I am sure we would have all died
that day. The men and I all went in for a swim

except your father. He was never able to relax even when it seemed like everything was going good. It was a damn good thing he was that way."

"I still don't know where they came from but when I looked there was your father surrounded by at least 20 Xyles. It was like they had been watching us the whole time. That was the first time we realized that they weren't just attacking randomly. We always just figured they were big dumb animals that migrated this way. Anyway, your father was doing okay for himself but we did not know how long he could keep it up, and we were not going to sit there and find out. Sill, he was the first one of us out of the water."

"He put on his pants and grabbed his sword in one motion and the rest of us were not too far behind him. There were only 10 of us of to the 20 of them but it still did not seem fair to them with your father there. For some reason, they were going after your father, and the ones who weren't going after him were trying to keep us from getting to him. As the fight went on, it became more fierce than we could have ever imagined. The more Lackshin killed, the more of them came out of the woods. The men and I noticed that they were all forming around your father as if they knew who he was.

"We all started to attack more of them ourselves to try to keep them off your father as best we could. Your father saw what the men and I were doing and fought through the best of them and ran away. I guess your father figured the men should fight for themselves instead of him.

Before the clearing your father made closed, Sill made it through and followed your father. Although, before he did that, he said something that made me think. Sill with such anger yelled, 'How dare they, how dare they ignore me! I'm just as great, if not greater than Lackshin.'"

Thrant paused for a moment, remembering his past all to well. "After that, all we have is their story as to what happened next, and that story is much more interesting. Your father ran off with those things right on his tail. He said he made it to a clearing in the woods where he stopped. They must have believed your father was running from them, instead he was just relocating to a better spot. He turned with sword in hand, with that same smirk I see on your face every time you pull your sword too. It is just amazing how much you are like your father."

"Yes, but your father was much bigger then you are, you are just a little guy," Ralyn said with a grin on his face.

"Look, we are here and it looks like the girls did not burn down my house," Ralyn said with a huge sigh of relief.

"Sanch, Menis, come on! We have to get you boys fed so you can get on your way," Thrant said sounding concerned.

Sanch quickly spoke up. "Are you not going to finish the story?"

Thrant replied, "The girls are going to need to hear the rest of this story so that they better understand what they are getting into if they decide to go with you on your quest. I'm not even sure that you are well aware of what you

have gotten yourself into. Don't get me wrong, I
have no doubt in my mind that you're the man
for the job, but the others unlike you were not
born for this. You need to know the enemy of
your father is an evil force that you alone can
stop. Sanch, do you know that your father left
you the tools with which to do so?"

After saying that, they followed Ralyn into
his home.

Chapter Eight

*When they entered the house, it seemed like
they entered a castle. It was not a very large house,
but its contents were that of royalty. There were
exquisite paintings on the walls of places and things
neither Sanch nor Menis had ever seen before.
There was also a sword hanging on the wall the
likes of which they had never seen anything before.
The sword had a ruby in the center of the handle
that looked a lot like an eye. The handle itself
looked like it was designed to fit the hands of the
user. The blade was not of a silver shade but a
white blade that looked to have never been used.*

"Where did you get such a sword, it's the greatest I have ever seen?" Menis blurted out.

"It was my father's sword that he passed down to me as I will to Bethany," Rayln said with pride.

"But it does not hold the power to vanquish Sillack like the sword of Lackshin does," Rayln said, reassure the boys and hopping to get a look at this sword they all have put their hopes in.

"Sanch, do you know why the blade of your father's sword is black?" Thrant asked.

"No, I just assumed that the time spent in the volcano turned it that way. Why? Is that not the case?"

"I'll let you know over dinner kid, let's go sit down."

They continued on through the house to the dining area where they saw Lisha balancing a loaf of bread on her sword. And there was Bethany, taking aim with her crossbow. Not noticing that they were being watched, they carried on with their act.

Menis just shrugged his shoulders and made his way over to the dinner table. As he got closer to the table he noticed that the table was made of marble, something you could not obtain easily. The chairs had blue velvet cushions and crafted legs. Menis, being from a warrior clan was not accustomed to such things; he ate most of his meals on the ground. He was not sure if he was to actually sit down on these chairs.

With a welcoming voice Ralyn asked Menis, "Are you going to sit with us or are you going to eat standing up?" Continuing, he added, "Kess took out the good chairs when she heard you guys were coming, and look, Bethany saved

you a seat next to her."
Looking at Sanch Bethany spoke up. "That chair is for whomever desires to sit in it."

Menis, with a smile on his face, "Well I desire!"

"Well that's more like it my boy, you come have a seat. There, right next to my pretty little warrior," loudly spoken by an amused Ralyn.

It seemed like everyone but Bethany found that to be humorous; but Menis was able to get a smile out of the slightly red faced Bethany. Kess, who was indirectly told how handsome these young warriors were by the girls, found it that much more amusing. She then went on to let them all know they did not need their swords at the dinner table; the bread had already been sliced. She collected the weapons all but one, the sword known as Shallin.

"So is that the sword all the fuss is about. And why is it black like that? That's funny; I can see my face in the blade. What manner of steel is this?" an inquisitive Kess asked.

"Sanch, has it always been that way or did they do something to it?"

"I do not know, it was like this when I rescued it from the volcano. I just thought maybe it got like that from the heat and lava. I think Thrant would be the man to ask about that." Sanch looks to Thrant.

Thrant cleared his throat, "I guess this is a good a time as any to finish my story."

"What story is that?" asked Lisha.

"I was telling Sanch of this enemy you kids are going to face soon. This man, known as Sillack, was Sanch's fathers second in command at that time. He was known as Sill back then, and he was a hell-of-a-warrior, but greed, power and jealousy got the best of him. Sanch, I think I left off at Sill following your father into the woods. They were able to fight off the Xyles successfully with little to no damage to themselves. The two tired warriors sat down under a tree, and laughed about how easy that was. The two friends did not sit down for long, they both wanted to hurry back to the main fight where their men were fighting those hideous creatures.

"Your father and Sill started running back to the river where they could hear the men still engaged. They did not notice how deep in the woods they took the Xyles. The only thing on their minds now was getting back to their others. In their haste, Lackshin and Sill did not realize that they were not alone. An alert Lackshin asked, 'Did you hear that?'

'Hear what? I didn't hear a thing. What is it?'

'Shhh,' Lackshin motioned for them to get down. 'Just listen. Do you hear that?'

A now aware Sill whispered, 'Now that I hear. What is it?'

'If I knew what it was I would not be here on the ground next to you.

Lets make a run for it, the men need us, and so whatever it is it's just going to have to do without us.'

The two jumped to their feet and ran for it. Now on their minds were getting back to the battle quickly, and what the hell is that in the woods. They did not get far before they ran into a figure of a person, so they thought.

This person stood 5'8" dressed in black with a cloak draped over its face. The two men pulled their swords and took ground. They were ready for anything. They were going around or through this thing. Then it spoke, with a voice that seem to be coming from everywhere. It addressed them by name. It took them both by surprise that this whatever it was knew their names.

'Lackshin, you can put your sword away, so can you, Sill, there is no need for them here. Both now with empty hands and swords somehow back at their sides. Sill now angry straightened his back. 'What are you?!'

'You both desire something and I think I can help you both with. You need something to fulfill your destiny and all you   have now to do is ask me.'

'What do you mean all we have to do is ask? We just ask for something and you give it to us?' Sill asked as he took a step forward.

Lackshin quickly grabbed Sill shoulder pulling him back. 'That sounds just too easy to be worth anything.' Lackshin said adding to this conversation.

'Yes, all you have to do is ask for your deepest desire and it is yours to have,' this cloaked figure said trying to convince the two of his proposal.

'We have no time for this, the men need us and I am going to them. Thanks for your offer but we must be going now. Come Sill let's leave this place.'

'I assure you that your men are okay. You need not run off before telling me what it is that you want most of all, and it is yours.'

In Sill's heart the need for power was growing like a fire raging out of control. Unknowing to Lackshin Sill desired nothing more than to be greater than him, and he saw this as his chance to become just that. He knew he would have to be careful about how he would ask for what he wanted. He wanted not to sound like he was being power driven, and wanted the power for the wrong reason. The more he heard of what could be done for him the desire grew and grew. He just could not take it anymore, he had to say something, and he just could not let this opportunity pass him by. He had to do something.

'So you are telling us that you can grant us one desired wish, and it would be so?'

Lackshin alarmed, said, 'Sill, we do not know what this thing wants in return for his gift.

Something like this must come with a great price, it is not just going to give us this and walk away. There is something more to this than we can see!'

Sill, trying to convince Lackshin, pleaded his case, 'Let's give it a try and if the price is too high we can just walk away from him and his offer. We can just see if he can help us obtain things we might need to win this war.'

'So what do you say, do you want what I have to offer you?' the cloaked man asked the two warriors.

'Yes, we do!' Sill spoke up.

He then proceeded to tell this man of his desire to be the most powerful and unstoppable man on earth. He wanted nothing more than to have the power needed to stop the Xyles and their master from taking over the land. Sill was being sincere when he said he wanted to protect the people of the land. That was one of his true desires, he did want to make the land safe for everyone; but that would all soon change. The cloaked stranger informed Sill that he could not make him the most powerful man in the land, that is something he would have to obtain on his own. But he could make him unstoppable against mortal men and these things he would fight.

'That is an easy request, that for you is done. You are now just as you want to be, you are unstoppable.'

'Now for you, Lackshin, what is it that you want? What do you most desire and have not been able to obtain?'

Lackshin just stood there looking at this being in disbelief. He was still not convinced that this cloaked figure could actually do what he claimed. He did not see why he should let this thing, whose face he had yet to see, know what it is he desired.

'I am going back to my men. Sill, you can stay and talk to this, but I am going.'

As he started on his way, the cloaked figure appeared in front of his path.

Furious, Lackshin asked, 'What are you doing? Get out of my way or...'

The cloaked being asked, 'Or what, Lackshin, what are you going to do?'

Lackshin, being the man that he is, was not going to be stopped by this person he did not know. Lackshin reached for his sword.

'Lackshin, what are you doing?' shouted Sill.

Lackshin stopped and looked at Sill while springing back and at the same time drawing his sword. He threw his sword, blade first, at the head of the cloaked stranger. He caught the sword by the blade inches in front of the opening in the cloak. When he did this, his hand was exposed to the warriors. It looked like a human hand but there was no blood flowing from him after catching the sword by its blade.

Filled with passion and a hint of anger in his voice, 'You see that? That is my sword and it is a great sword, but by far not enough to stop my enemy. What I desire is a weapon that will vanquish my enemy and any evil that may threaten this land and the people who live freely here. I want a weapon that is true to me and my own, and cannot be tainted by any other hands. I want my son, if need be to have the strength to finish what I have started. I want Sanch to see peace in his lifetime more than anything.'

Lackshin enquired, 'Can you do this for me, can you do what you say?'

'What you ask for is going to take more time than your friend's request. This is going to have to be okayed by the other Gods, this is going to take some time.'

He threw the sword to the ground, putting the blade well into the ground. The stranger turned to depart, but then he stopped and spoke.

'I'm going to need something from you before I go.'

Before Lackshin knew what happened, the stranger was standing right in front of him. The stranger leaned in and spoke into his ear.

'To give you what you want I'm going to need something of yours. I'm going to need blood in order to give you what you want.'

'The stranger took out a knife donning a black blade of which Lackshin had not seen anything like before. He took the knife in one hand and Lackshin's hand in the other, and then he was gone. Not leaving a scar or spilling a drop of his blood. Lackshin retrieved his sword and then they agreed to speak of this with no one outside the men back at the camp. These twenty men back at the camp are the only ones that could be trusted with this kind of information. I, Sanch was one of the twenty men that heard the tale first hand. After hearing what Sill said before pursuing your father made me question his reason for what he asked for. Your father on the other hand asked for just what he needed to bring this war to an end. With Shallin he did just that. It was weeks before he was given the sword; he was even beginning to doubt the stranger's promise. Then one day, out of nowhere a dragon swooped down and carried your father away. When he came back he had Shallin and the tide was turned. All the time before Shallin became an ally, Sill was becoming more and more powerful. Yet he was never able to better Lackshin even with his new power. What your father had naturally was unreachable by average men, and that angered Sill to no end. He was better than all the other men, but that was not enough for Sill."

"Are you boys going to eat, or is the talk of that sword going to fill your bellies?" Kess asked as she took a seat at the table.

"You boys have done nothing but speak of this sword. You Sanch, by the sound of things do not have that much time to waste before you are off again. I feel you should do less talking and more eating as you are going to need your strength. If you are to save us you are going to have to put a little meat on those bones. Besides, don't you want to get some sleep before leaving on your journey?" A concerned Kess enquired.

Noticing something the others knew not of, Lisha was going to make known.

"Sanch does not sleep."

A now informed Thrant looked to Lisha with a face of question. "And how is that, that you know this? He bent down when we did."

As this conversation went on, Sanch continued to eat his food. He said nothing to confirm or deny any of what was being said. He was clearly taking Kess's advice and went on with his meal. Besides, no one included him so he saw no reason to intervene.

"I found it strange that Sanch was always the first one up in the morning, so one night I stayed up. To my surprise he went off far enough so he would not wake us, but never too far to where he could not see us. There he spent the night getting to know Shallin. Just from what I was able to see he was born to wield her."

"No Lisha that sword was born to be in his hand. Only there can Shallin show us her true power."

"Are you going to start in on that sword once again Thrant as my dinner gets cold?"

"No Kess," Thrant replied directing his eyes down at his food.

"I am done speaking of this sword. By the way, this is delicious, what is it?" Thrant said trying to keep clear of Kess and her wrath.

Chapter Nine

At the same time on the other side of the land Shallin was also the main topic of conversation. In a far off place, a dark castle stood where it seemed like the sun never shined. The castle was surrounded by molten lava that seemed to bleed from the earth's core. It had what looked like demons on horses patrolling the perimeter of the castle, and that was the first line of defense.

"How is it that they let that boy obtain Shallin? I want every one of them brought to me and killed!" A great voice echoed off the walls. "I want them to die slowly for letting Shallin be taken from me!"

"That is going to be impossible my lord."

"And why is that?" He asked with the sound of his chalice hitting the ground.

With his hand on his chest, he cleared his throat trying to hide the quiver in his voice. "Sanch has already killed them all inside the volcano when he came for the sword."

"When will Alshin be returning with Sanch and the traitor Thrant? I am growing impatient with all this. I want them brought to me now with Shallin, you know not what that sword can do in the hands of that boy!"

"Yes Sillack, I will get right on it. They will be in your grasp before you know it my lord. I will get word to Alshin on the arrangements of his task."

As he entered his throne room he shouted back. "I will hold you to that."

Sillack slammed the two steel doors leading to the throne room, leaving his second in command Haygen standing before closed doors. Haygen now with his life in the balance turned and went storming through the castle making his way to the courtyard. He shouted to all his troops to gather around him, and in his voice they could tell there was going to be hell to pay. When they all assembled and were in formation he informed them of the task at hand and picked his fastest rider and told him on what had to be done. He was sent to Alshin and his men to tell them of Sillack's demands.

"Tell Alshin that there will be no failing this task, because failure means death. He must bring Sanch alive with Shallin to Sillack, or he may as well take his own life. Let him know to do everything in his power to not fail. And if he fails at this to not let me find him for that will be an even bigger mistake. And as for you, I need you to ride non stop until you get there as there is no time to waste."

Through the little window in his throne room Sillack looked on as his men gathered in his name. He saw that things were as he foresaw them to be. He had become far more powerful than Lackshin had ever been. He saw that men, his men feared him more then death itself. They would rather walk through fire than turn and face him and his sword.

"If Lackshin could only see how powerful I have become in spite of his efforts to stop me," spoken boldly, a proud Sillack said as he looked on over his shoulder.

From one of the darkest corners of this room came a deep demonic voice that seemed to fill the room with a cold chill. This voice spoke of Shallin and her power, and the respect she should be given. He also spoke of Sanch and his coming and the power he himself will bring.

"What will you do when Sanch gets here, you do know he will have Shallin with him? And I do not think you need to send for him. If you wait long enough he will, I'm sure, find you."

"What makes you think he will ever make it here unescorted by my men? You are right Sanch will make it here, but on my terms we will meet."

Sillack looked out to the courtyard still trying to make clear of the challenge ahead, and the danger that soon approached. The voice continued on its campaign.

"Do you think Sanch will be as simple to defeat as his father was? He has only one thing on his mind and that is to kill you; the man he watched kill his father."

Sillack turned and pulled his sword and stepped towards the darkness where the voice radiated from. He imbedded the tip of his sword into the blackness.

"This sword killed his father and if he does not join me this sword will kill him too. His father could not stop me, and he is not the warrior that his father was."

"I was there Sillack and Lackshin held back when you two fought, but I do not think Sanch will do the same. As for his skills as a warrior, Shallin can give him all the edge he may need to carry out his desire to kill you. I think you know what needs to be done to ensure that you keep your seat on that throne of yours. There is only one way I see to assure your eternal reign as king of all the lands you wish to rule. And the destruction of the one you wish to destroy."

Wanting to know how to keep this power, a power he killed indiscriminatively to obtain. He desired this power more then anything, even more so than friendship.

"Tell me wizard, what do you see as the solution to my Sanch problem? Besides killing him or making him an ally of my case."

"We let the Xyles bring him back to us."

"And I guess you will control them as well as you did when Lackshin and I had to defeat them? Can they even think for themselves, or are we going to unleash non-thinking killing beasts on the lands once again?"

"They where always under my control until I just wanted you all dead at all cost. That's when they acted with no restraints."

"If we do this, they will listen to me and only me. I let you live because I felt you might serve some purpose. Do not make me sorry. I let you keep your other eye or this time I will take your head."

"If we are to do this, we should get started on summoning them from their evil place of rest. I am sure that it will not be as hard to control them as it had been the last time I brought them to my aid in my battle against you and Lackshin." He boasted of his campaign and it's reign of terror.

Curious Sillack enquired of his reasons behind his madness.

"Why is it that you waged war on us, people who had done you no wrong? You let those things loose on the land and gave us no choice but to fight. I was the son of a farmer that had to take up arms and fight to keep the land safe from an enemy we could not beat. Do you have any idea what your madness cost us; me and the friends I lost?"

A crystal patch covered his eye, reflected what little light that was allowed into the room. The wizard stepped into the light.

"And the friends you've killed. We can stand here and speak of the past and the wrong we've done. I think it would be in our best interest to get started before Sanch is knocking at the doors to this throne room. And then it will be to late for us to do anything about it, he will surely take your throne."

"Yes but not before I take your head; you will not live to see that happen. It is in your best interest to make sure that does not happen for you will see death before I do. Now, where do we find this kind of evil that you are to release once again on the land?"

"Not the land, on Sanch and whom ever chooses to die with him. We must first wait until nightfall to release this kind of evil. The time in which they are more comfortable showing themselves, therefore, that is when we will go for them. If you did not notice they did come out in the daytime, but they were fiercer at night. That is when they did most of their damage and their more gruesome killings."

"I know what they are capable of, they were fierce in the day and damn near unstoppable at night. Those things were unforgiving to anyone in their path, and just as merciless in their killing of the innocent people that stood in their way. Know this, I have in my days come to see that no one is truly innocent, we have all had our share of wrong," Sillack stated as he walked toward the two steel doors.

"No matter, we make our way to this place at dusk. Make certain that you can do as you say you can or that other eye of yours will be mine, and I will put it with the other. I do look forward to seeing what you can really do. It again would be in your best interest to not fail me in this task. Do be on time, I hate to be left waiting," he said, as the door slammed behind him.

Sillacks loud footsteps filled the halls as he made his way to his chambers.

As Sillack made his way to his private room he could not help but to think of the past. He remembered being second best to Lackshin when he should have been leading. As he thought of Lackshin and his victories he became enraged. He became more and more convinced that what he was doing had to be done to ensure his reign over the land. Having his power was all that mattered to him, and there were no lengths to which he was not willing to go. If that meant releasing such evil on the land once again, then he planned to do just that.

It was now dusk and like Sillack suggested the wizard was indeed on time. He in no way wanted to disappoint Sillack for that indeed would cost him his life. The men who were accompanying them were hard at work preparing Sillack's Rinnis for his travel. This animal was like no other, it was bred especially for Sillack and only Sillack could ride it. The beast stood 6' and was taller than any seen before. It was jet black with a straggly dog-like tail, which is not how they were known to grow. The animal's eyes glowed a haunting red, and emitted a slight ray, striking even his men as strange. It was being said that this thing, this beast, was given to Sillack by the Devil himself. The hooves were like no other Rinnis they were more like the paws of a predator. It had razor sharp claws and that they found to be the oddest thing about it. As they prepared the beast, its master arrived. Sillack dressed in his armor entered the stable not making a sound. He stood there in the shadow blending into the blackness, a glare radiated from his polished chest and that made him look much more fierce. He stood there undetected shielded in the black, his shoulders erected looking on. Dressed in such heavy armor, Sillack should have made more noise than he did. He moved around in silence as if his feet did not touch the ground, but floated on thin air; yet he left his mark everywhere he stepped. His armor almost perfectly contoured to his body still giving him full range of motion, and all while giving him full protection. On his forearm were blades that curved upwards making them deadly weapons in battle. As the men were preparing his Rinnis, one of them cut their hands on its saddle buckle, not a bad cut but it was enough to make him bleed. Just as the skin broke and the blood was exposed the Rinnis went wild. It smelled the blood and it put the beast into a rage. This rage was not one ever seen from such a beast. Yes they were known as fierce animals, yet even this was not expected. It threw the other two men off to the other side of the stable.

Sillack remained in the shadows and watched on as his men were being thrown around by this beast, and did nothing to restrain his enraged beast and help his men. After it threw the two men it turned its attention to the man whose arm was now covered in blood. The Rinnis growled as it approached the fallen stable hand. Its eyes where now glowing a bright red, its nose flared and teeth were all showing; it was clear that harm was to come to this man. With her mouth salivating she slowly approached. She lowered her body to the ground as she moved in closer. The man, frozen with fear, was cornered and had nowhere to escape. He reached for his sword, but just as he did she went for his arm. Her teeth with no mercy clamped down like a vise grip severing his limb. A scream of extreme pain rang out from the barn, and echoed through the castle. The Rinnis was now tossing this man around like a rag doll until he ripped his arm from his body leaving a bloody pulp were his arm once hung. And Sillack still just looked on as one of his men were torn apart, and the others were throw about. He stood there and did nothing to assist them. He dawned a familiar smile, one that had been seen on Sanch's face once before. The other two men rushed to their feet and drew their sword to try and stop the raging beast. As they approached, a voice was heard that seemed to shake the ground on which they where standing. This was a familiar voice, one that could indeed bring their lives to a sudden end.

"What exactly are you two planning on doing with those swords and my Rinnis? I'll give you one suggestion, holster your weapons, pick up your friend there and clean him up. Oh yes, and where is that wizard of mine?" Sillack asked, slightly irate.

"I think he is outside awaiting your arrival my lord."

"You may want to get him patched up before he bleeds to death all over my barn. I will finish preparing my friend here as soon as she is done with her meal."

He prepared the beast and just as the men stated, the wizard was outside the barn waiting for him. The wizard was riding a full white horse, a horse as white as newly fallen snow. The men who where chosen to accompany them on this quest for unholy evil were also there. They were anxiously awaiting Sillack's emergence from the stable riding his unholy steed. The men all heard thunder, then the doors to the barn flew open and emerged Sillack on his hell-bred steed. All the horses lowered their heads and backed up out of its path. The men looked on in amazement at this beast that let out a roar that filled the courtyard. When she touched down and her claws hit the stone covered ground, sparks shot from the claws on its feet.

"Wizard, I am glad to see that you made it on time, I was afraid that I might have been forced to kill you. Now all you have to do is show me that you can do what you say, and you get to live a little longer. Now men, if you are all here and ready we can see what it is this wizard has in store for us."

Sillack slid down his face shield, turned to the wizard and gave him a nod.

"Shall we depart now wizard?"

They rode off in the direction of what seemed to be a bright reddish orange sphere partly submerged in the ground. It was setting as if to mark a new reign of evil to come. Just like Sillack, the darkness swept across the land leaving everything in its path covered in gloom. Unknown to Sillack, his wizard had other plans in mind for the evil they were about to release. He held malice, and in no way wanted to see Sillack succeed where he failed. They have now been riding for an hour and he is taking them the long way, giving himself time to come up with a plan in which to eventually take over control of the Xyles.

Angered, "How much further wizard? We have been riding for an eternity! The men and I are holding in our excitement to see your great power that is so well renown."

"Not much longer my lord, just through the dark forest and the cave should be on the other side. The cave where they returned to when you and Lackshin banished them." The Wizard now out of time replied.

And under his breath he uttered, "If it were not for Shallin and Lackshin, my victory would have been complete."

"To say that again will cost you your life, be sure to remember that wizard. Speak not of Lackshin or that sword, they are nothing compared to me! I proved that not even Lackshin and that sword could stop me."

"Yes my lord, I will make no more mention of them."

Not long after that, they came to the edge of the forest. As they approached, the horses started slowing down. It became now difficult to convince the horses to press on. What was in the darkness, these were battle harden animals that were now scared to the point of not moving. Sillack's Rinnis seemed to feel right at home in this evil that surrounded this unholy place. The other animals seemed to not want to continue on.

"Get those beasts under control and follow me! Any man who does not enter this forest will see first hand the point on my blade so stand ready; who knows what we might find in here?"

There were battle cries sounded and horses reared and Sillack and his men mercilessly penetrated the forest, for it was to be done. Hearing that said, the wizard found himself donning a smirk for he knew for sure that there were dangerous creatures lurking in the dark. He was hoping that one of them might kindly dispose of Sillack for him, and save him the trouble of having to do it himself. As they galloped through the trees trying to avoid what might be lurking in the dark, one of the men, before he knew it was snatched from his horse. The horse realized what had happened and started galloping past the others. One of the other men noticed what happened and that one of the riders was gone.

"Where the hell did he go?" he shouted.

The wizard knowing what was going on was not at all surprised, and keeps riding until he hears a cry.

"Stop!" shouted Sillack, the loud sound of steal scraping on the inside of a wooden sheath broke the silence. Sillack pulled his sword from its place of rest. "Where is that horses rider? Did he not enter the forest? Wizard what is going on, is this your doing?"

The wizard replied, "We all knew that there were strange things inhabiting this place before we entered. Come now, the longer we stay still the more chances we give them to attack us again, whatever they are. We would do good to be moving targets as opposed to sitting ducks."

"Move out!" shouted Sillack to the men who remained. "Wizard lead the way, I want to keep you in my sight. For if I remember correctly, this was at one time your dwelling place, and where your power was the strongest. No matter, just don't forget I will not hesitate to separate your head from your body at any time."

"Ya!" shouted the wizard who rode off with Sillack and his men close behind. Not long after starting back on their way one of the men saw something moving up ahead.

"What is that?" Sillack wailed, sweeping his eyes back and forth through the darkness.

"What did you see?"

"Look, its moving over there. Can you see it my lord?"

A familiar look came over Sillack's face. It was like he saw something of a haunting sight; a sight he did not miss.

"Isn't that a...?"

Suddenly they were surrounded by green beams glowing in at them from the blackness. He knew it could be nothing other than Xyles looking in at them. It was like they appeared from nowhere, and were now everywhere you looked. The wizard was not afraid for he knew they would not harm him.

"Sillack, what are we going to do, they are everywhere?"

Sillack once again gave a familiar smirk and lowered his visor as he dismounted his Rinnis. He stepped down as his men looked on wondering what he was doing. The men stayed on their horses, because they had never seen the likes of this manner of beast before. They knew not what they should expect from these creatures that were now surrounding them. It was clear that the alpha male was the one in front blocking their path, challenging Sillack's passing. As the others lunged back and forth as if to herd the men into a controlled state he asked, "What should we do my lord?"

"Just stay where you are I'll deal with the big one; and I don't think the others are going to be too anxious to join in when I'm finished with him. In fact, I think I know this one from times long past. He will quickly remember me when I am finished here and he will know just who I am."

"What are you planning on doing?" The wizard enquired.

He asked as Sillack approached the beast with no sword in hand. That to the wizard seemed like suicide, but Sillack's death would give him just what he wanted. The power and the possibility of power was all that the wizard had on his mind. As for Sillack; he had blood in his eyes and the desire to kill something, and the Xyles was what he had in mind. He approached the beast with no sword in hand and it was clear that he was going to take this one apart with his bare hands. The whole time, his Rinnis was not too far behind him, unlike the horses, she showed no fear. Yet like the horses, the men where glued to their saddles by fear. Other than the growling from the Xyles, the forest was silent. The men looked on as Sillack closed in on his clearly larger opponent that seemed more than prepared to receive him. But was he? As his soldiers looked on, the moon glistened off the freshly polished armor of one of Sillack's young warriors. It gave the same glimmer that you would see reflecting off a slowly rippling lake.

His armor had clearly never seen the tarnish of battle, or the taint of war and its way of destruction. The young warrior had only trained for such things, but had never seen such evil in physical form as he did now. He only knows of the creatures from the whispers of bedtime stories told by his mother; but they were always happy endings. The stories always ended with a hero called Lackshin who with the help of a mystical black blade drove the evil back to the hell from whence they came, but he is no longer.

The young warrior showed fear in his face, yet stood ready for what would occur. He looked to one of the men who were clearly experienced in the art of war. He had his sword drawn and a prepared look on his face, and he showed no fear. His armor was tarnished and riddled with dents and stained with blood. His sword strangely enough was clean and extremely sharp. He turned to the old warrior with obvious fear in his eyes. He tried to hide it but experienced eyes passed through his cover.

"Don't worry, it will be over fast, you won't even see them coming. You just have to be ready when they get here."

"What do you mean? What is to come of us? What chance do we really have against these beasts?"

"We will most likely be killed by the owners of the eyes you see glaring at us. Just be glad that the eyes are all you see, for the evil that has assembled around us, is like none I assure you boy, that your nightmares could manifest."

"So what are we doing here if we knew these things would be here? Why would Sillack bring us here knowing that we would encounter such things?"

"With the look of pity in his eyes, he leaned in closer to the boy. Sillack was doing the unthinkable; he was there to undo the work Lackshin and so many other brave men fought and died to accomplish. And Sillack is going to change all that. He is going to unleash hell on earth, and I fear it will be much worse than the last time."

"But why would he do such a thing? What is he trying to accomplish by doing this? He must fear nothing if he's to do this."

"Fear is exactly the force that brought us here. Think there is someone he fears more than these things you see around us?"

"What could possibly bring him to this?"

"Not what--but who. The man whose work tonight we are to undo, was stopped by his belief in friendship, but he did give us something to hope for. He left us his son, and I don't think he will be as forgiving as his father was. Shhh, look, Sillack's about to kill or be killed."

As they looked up they saw Sillack looking up into green glowing eyes. They looked closer and they could see the silhouette of the Xyles glaring down at Sillack.

Chapter Ten

The beast slowly stepped out from the shadow; light flowed over him like water over a rock revealing the true face of evil. It was by far the fiercest creature this young warrior had ever seen.

"What the hell is that?"

"That, my young man, is what your nightmares will be of if you are lucky enough to live through this. Just be ready for anything. These demons show no mercy and neither should you; so keep your eyes open and your wits about you. It looks like this is going to get messy."

The beast emerged from the dark with confidence—and why not? Here stood a man half its size with no weapon in his hand. Looking around, he saw terrified men on horseback, too afraid to get down. He sees this as no challenge; these men are no threat. With his hands stretched out on either side of him he leaned back and lunged his head forward letting out a blood-curdling roar at an attempt to intimidate Sillack. The horses reared nearly throwing some of the men. The young warrior now saw reason to draw his sword.

Sillack's men who were stationed near the forest heard the spine-shattering roar of this hell-born beast. The old warrior heard it as a sound he did not think he would live long enough to hear again, but here it was as heinous as he remembered it to have been. He knew that tonight life would be given to new nightmares. He himself knew he would be lucky if life graced him to see another day and partake of the nightmares that so generously would be handed out this night. The alpha Xyle relaxed its shoulders and summoned back the evil it so generously bestowed, Sillack stood unmoved as so his Rinnis would remain at his side. Sillack found it nothing more than amusing and showed that with his outburst of laughter.

"These Xyles are just as I remember them. They will make a great addition to my army."

The Xyle and the Xyles looking on did not find the same humor that Sillack expressed. The alfa showed it with his next show of aggression. The beast raised his right arm and with a growl took an attempt at Sillack's head. Before Sillack could react his Rinnis caught the beast by the wrist with his sharpened teeth; clamping down splashing blood on Sillack's armor. Sillack looked at his Rinnis with the wrist of this large Xyle in his mouth.

"You have a thing for arms don't you?" he asked as he shrugged his shoulders, while his Rinnis bit down.

"Sure why not? You can have it."

As he said that, the beast lost his arm from the shoulder to the equally vicious Rinnis. The Xyles, letting out a roar that once again woke up the hillside, and the people that inhabited it. Sillack decided his Rinnis should not be the only one allowed to have fun, and decided to take part in the dismembering. He clinched his fist and with that deployed a blade from the armor located on the back of his forearm. With one slash to the Xyles midsection, he revealed its inners spilling its insides to the ground. The young warrior witnessed this and could not believe what he was seeing: such a beast being taken apart by a man and his Rinnis. After seeing what Sillack was capable of, he felt a little more confident that he would live through this ordeal. Just when it looked like the worst was over, the congregation of Xyles that surrounded them, backed up slowly and the glow of green distinguished by the darkness. Suddenly the roar that was heard from the alpha Xyle was now surrounding them, then there was just silence. All of a sudden the glow returned, but this time it was radiating from above.

"There, in the trees!" shouted the young man who noticed their relocation.

"To arms men, to arms!" Shouted Sillack.

The unprepared soldiers reached for their swords and the young warrior stood ready with sword in hand. The haunting glow of green eyes was now closing in on them. The Xyles were jumping down from the trees. One of the beasts went for the young warrior, but like the old man said he did not see it coming.

"Look out boy!" blared the old man.

The young man turned and with one swipe of his sword took the head of a Xyle that landed right in front of him, splattering blood over both him and his older brother in arms. In spite of the blood that was now on him, the old warrior gave a nod of approval to the young man who clearly knew how to use a sword. Even Sillack, as he ran back to join the men as they were fighting for their lives, noticed the skill this warrior possessed. He and the others jumped down from the horses; they felt they would have a better chance on the ground. One warrior was caught off guard and killed. His head was pulled back and the Xyles ripped his throat out with his teeth. The beast kept hold of the man's head as his body convulsed, and with his other hand he tore through his armor and pulled out his heart. He simply disposed of the lifeless body in a pool of his own blood as the rest of the men helplessly looked on. The young warrior chose not to stand around and look on as they killed everyone around him. He was not going to die today, not at the hands of these things.

"It will not end here, I will not die tonight; not when my sword still has a blade!" declared the young man.

The other men heard his cry and agreed they also were not ready to die at the hands of these abominations sent from hell. The men all dug in and gripped firmly to their swords, and simply put forth a fight, earning the right to live another day. There was a lot of blood shed after his battle cry, but this time it was the blood of the Xyles being spilled. You can be certain that most of the blood was on the sword of Sillack whom you could tell took pleasure in the contribution to the killing of his old enemies.

"Wizard, stand there and do nothing and when I am finished here I will kill you myself." Sillack made known.

The wizard uttered some words that vibrated off his lips and rode the winds. The remaining Xyles fell helpless, started backing away giving the men the upper hand. Sillack stepped down on one of the beasts face; you could hear bones breaking as he dislodged his sword from its chest. He flipped up his visor and his red glowing eyes glared at the wizard who knew not the danger his life was now in.

"I should kill you for just looking on as my men fought for their lives. If I did not know better one would think you wanted us to lose that fight. Lucky for you I need you or this sword would also be stained with your blood."

Sillack bellowed as his eyes faded slowly back to his normal color. The other men looked at the wizard with disgust and anger; some slightly injured and all fatigued--the men gathered themselves some still in shock prepared to press on, their numbers greatly diminished. The young man turned to the old warrior, "Are you OK? I lost sight of you during the battle. You're not injured are you?"

"You son, I did not lose sight of, you are quite the warrior. Are you sure you were not born with a sword in your hand? You might not have seen them coming, but you were ready when they got there. Your sword is now crimsoned with blood and none of yours spilled; you are a warrior to be reckoned with. Your lord Sillack is looking over here, I am not the only one that has noticed skills my boy.”

Sillack ordered the remaining men to mount up and prepare to move out. He rode his Rinnis over to the young warrior and glared down at him with a look of approval. The fatigued warrior with blood still wet on his hands gripped the reins and was going to mount his horse but stopped to acknowledge his leaders presence.

“So boy, what do they call you?”

“I am Taddayuse. I am from Tegra, my lord,” he humbly replied.

“I have not seen you before. You are very skilled with that sword. Now that we have met I will be keeping an eye on you and your progress.” Raising his voice he now was addressing the others as well. “For now men, we move out, we don’t have much further to go, is that not so wizard?”

“Yes my lord; if my memory serves me correctly it should be just up ahead through this darkness. That is most likely why the Xyles attacked us as they did, they were protecting the resting place of the others.”

“Attacked us? It seemed like you were out of harms-way, and we were being cut down as you looked on. I have the mind to cut your head from your body!” angrily shouted Taddayuse as he reached for his sword.

"Stand down!" Sillack firmly said. "Taddayuse, he still has to take us where we are going, and he is the only one who knows where that is. So unfortunately we have to keep him alive, for now."

Sillack rode up next to the wizard, his Rinnis towering over the wizard and his horse.

"You would be wise to keep that one good eye of yours on your friend there. Rest assured that he will now be watching you, you have seen him with a sword and I'm sure you know he can make true with his threat. No harm is to come to him or I will see that his threat is made true." Sillack whispered to the wizard.

With a motion of his head Sillack gave the OK for the wizard to lead the way. As they made their way into the darkness, the young Taddayuse rode closely to the wizard as to keep an eye on him. As they approached it seemed to separate one side of the forest from the other, the sounds seemed to lessen. The dark that the wizard was referring to was like none that Taddayuse had ever seen. It was a consuming blackness clocked them like the armor they wore. It seemed to swallow up everything around it and let nothing escape. It felt like it would eventually get too thick for even them to pass through; like a shroud that separated the evil from the most evil. The horses held back as they knew that there was nothing but wrong from this point on. The men also could tell that they should not go any further, but defying Sillack would mean dying anyway. At least this way they had a fighting chance with what dwelled in the dark.

Taddayuse dropped back to have word with the old warrior that befriended him. Taddayuse unsure to what was going on. Shoulders bouncing with the trot of the horse; he leans in so not to be heard by the others.

"Do you know why Sillack would bring us to such a place, I just don't see what we would be doing here. Or what could be gained from an evil place such as this." Taddayuse whispered under his breath.

"No, I do not know what is to come of this, but I do know one thing: no good will come of this." The seasoned warrior replied.

"If this is where Lackshin put them, then there is no reason for us to be here; there is nothing here for us to do." A confused Taddayuse said as he pulls on the reins keeping the horses close.

"There is only one thing we could be doing here, and that is one of the reasons the wizard needs to be here." He told Taddayuse as he taps the beast with his heals to keep pace.

"And what is that?" Taddayuse enquires.

Just then everything came to a halt. Taddayuse looked up and saw a cave shaped like an eye, a strange heat radiated off the rocks and the cave itself. In the center there was the most amazing sight to ever be seen by Sillack and all his men, yet the wizard did not seem surprised by this sight. Before them in the center of this eye was a swirl of not only fire but of water as well, it was like it was looking at them, never blinking; seeing all. It was the most amazing thing, the fire and water was intertwined perfectly. You could not tell where the water stopped and the fire began. The water was just as the fire was, burning in an almost blinding blasé of red hints of orange and the blue of the water burning in a intertwining assortment of colors. If you looked closely in the center of all this, you could see a ruby spinning amongst all the chaos.

"What is this wizard, is this another of one of your tricks?"

"Take a good look." The wizard replied. "This is a sample of the power that Shallin holds. This is what you can expect—and possibly much more when Sanch learns to use his father's sword."

Taddyuse climbed down from his horse and walked in closer to better see things and what was going on. The ruby spun in the center of the eye, being sustained by seemingly nothing. It spun well under control like if on an axis. The wizard, as if in a trance, for the first time on the journey, came down from his horse. In this trance, he did not notice Taddyuse staying close, watching his every move. The wizard walked slowly towards the eye. Taddyuse heard him mumble something under his breath. At first not being able to fully make out what he said.

Power to Rule

"Behind this eye of magic holds the power to rule this land, or if I see fit—the power to destroy it all. My creatures will once again know destruction and the taste of blood."

Drawing his sword, Taddayuse turned to the wizard, placing his sword to his throat.

"Not if I kill you first wizard. Those things were put there for a reason, and I feel that they should remain there."

Sillack, not looking around or turning to see what was taking place behind him, spoke.

"Taddayuse, I like you, but I'm not going to tell you again. Stand down. I told you that I still need him to get me what I want. And what I want is on the other side of this eye, and Taddayuse, we are here to meet my new army."

With a look of horror and disbelief on his unshaved bloodstained face, Taddayuse stumbled back.

"We are here to do what?" His breathing became heavy, his shoulders raised and dropped aggressively, he griped firmly his already drawn sword.

"Do you have a problem with that Boy?"

The old warrior hurried off his horse and rushed to Taddayuse's side.

"No my lord! He has no quarrels with your intentions to open the eye."

"Good, because you two will be joining the wizard and myself through to the other side. Taddayuse I want you to keep an eye on him." As Sillack rested his hand on the wizard's shoulder. "I need him but just as you I do not trust him." Sillack slowly applied pressure.

"You Daren, you can get us through this can you not?" Sillack asked the wizard.

"There is only one way to know this." The wizard Daren replied.

He then stepped out away from the others and extended his arms. In his right hand he held a full black staff with a jagged crystal secured by what seemed to resemble a claw. The wizard started to speak in strange tongue that to Taddayuse seemed like an assortment of mumbled words. Trees were now being disturbed by the increasing winds that were blowing through the darkness. The young man looked out and saw the green glowing eyes of the Xyles that escaped his sword at their last meeting. Lightning split a tree in half, which had set some of the horses off not too far from where he was standing. Taddayuse turned his attention to the wizard and looked on as he attempted to dilate the eye. You could see the anticipation building in Sillack as he looked on, getting closer to the army he feels will help him defeat Sanch and the sword called Shallin.

Fillip stayed close to Taddayuse, his sword firmly in his hand in the event it may be needed to defend. The other men stayed back on their horses making sure not to come too close. Sillack's Rinnis, to no one's surprise stayed close to her master's side. With his visor still down you could see the glow of red building in Sillack's eyes due to his excitement as well as the evil growing in his heart. As the eye became more and more dilated the ring of fire and water spun faster and faster. The ruby that was spinning fast was slowing down to where its shape was revealed. The ruby began to glow hot and shone brightly.

Sillack clutched his fist in anticipation. As the ruby became brighter Sillacks eyes began glowing bright red. Taddayuse could feel the power building in both Sillack and the ruby, yet he could

"Taddayuse, hold your ground; this evil you
feel. Keep this feeling and hold it and embed it in
your memory. You will feel this again; this evil and
much more evil before this is over. More than you
will think you can stand, but you must always stand
your ground and face it and see it for what it is: A
reign that needs to be stopped, a heat that needs to
be cooled."

The aroma of evil continued to build, as
Taddayuse stood ready for whatever might emerge
from this cave filled with evil magic. This went on
for a long time; the wizard chanted on until the eye
was open enough for us to pass through. The ruby
was now moving at just a slow rotation; its shape
was now clear. It was strangely shaped like a claw,
a claw that every man there now knew too well. It
was the claw of one of the beasts that just attacked
them; a Xyles claw but made of ruby. Like nothing
that Taddayuse or the other men including Sillack
had seen before. The wizard fell to his knees from
the exhaustion of using so much magic, and was left
being held by his staff. Expelling that much magic
could have killed the wizard but instead brought
him to his knees. Sillack walked over and put his
hand on the wizard's shoulder once again. "You did
good, but do not die just yet, I may still need you
for something more. Now get to your feet; we don't
have time for you to rest. You can rest when the boy
kills you."

With the glow of red subsiding in his eyes, "Taddayuse you and your companion bring your swords, you will need them."

"Wizard! What now, do we just walk in?"

The wizard, pulling himself back to his feet with his staff had little to no strength left, "You must take the ruby; that is what you must poses to control these creatures. Without it they would just kill everything and everyone they came across until there was nothing remaining of any of us. That is how I was able to control them the way that I did, until Lackshin figured that out and made it the way to defeat me. That sword of his made this ring of fire and water to keep out those who might want to undo what Lackshin had done. Once open, only the sword of Lackshin can return the Xyles to this place and return them to their sleep."

"Well, let's make sure that does not happen this time." Sillack said as he walked to the eye of fire and water.

Sillack reached out towards the slowly but still spinning ruby with his left hand for in his right hand was his sword just in case; he did not know what would happen once the claw was removed. Not far behind was his Rinnis. Sillack hesitated just for a second; he formed a tight fist and then released it. He leaned forward and closed that hand around the ruby. The red of the ruby glowed through Sillack's fingers. It seemed to just hang there even as he held it. You could tell by Sillacks movement that the ruby was not coming down without a fight.

"What is wrong with this thing?" Sillack shouted to the wizard who had the look of fear on his face. Sillack stuck his sword into the ground and covered his left hand with his right hand, and continued to pull with all his strength. Taddayuse not quite sure what was to become of all of them if he does manage to remove it. The wizard still looking extremely frightened; noticed the eye was beginning to close. Sillack with his full concentration on the ruby did not see that the eye was becoming proximal around him. Taddayuse, seeing what was happening, looked on trying to understand what was going on with the eye. When he saw enough and that the eye was still closing he ran over to the wizard. Placing his sword to his throat, "Don't just stand there; do something, the eye is closing around him; stop it."

"What are you asking of me? What am I to do?"

"If you do nothing I will kill you where you stand, and I think you know I will do it."

The more the eye closed the more noise the Xyles in the forest made. The men who stayed back became very uneasy; they could hear them moving in closer waiting for the opportunity to strike once again. The old warrior tried to get the men ready for a possible attack.

"Men stand fast. Those things are not going to stop this time until we are all dead or dying."

Taddayuse shouted back just as the old warrior did. "That is not going to happen, is it wizard? You're not going to let that happen, are you?"

Finally, noticing what was going on Sillack shouted. "Wizard what is going on and why is it that this thing is closing? And what is it that I am to do to remove this ruby from its place of rest?"

With Taddayuse's sword still at his throat he replied, "I do not know my lord. I just gathered that you would be able to remove it."

"You might want to come up with a better solution than that if I am to stop Taddayuse from removing your head from your body."

Having as much as he could take, an angered Sillack steps away from the eye and turns to see what was taking place behind him.

"How was it that Lackshin placed the ruby in this, and how was he planning to remove it?"

"I do not think he was planning to removing it from this place…as you put it my lord."

Sillack looked to Taddayuse. "Take his head if the eye starts to close again. Wizard, if you wish to keep your head you will open this eye and keep it that way; that ruby is coming with me even if it costs you your head."

The wizard being fully aware that Taddayuse would not hesitate to remove his head from his body. He agreed and started once more to chant. The eye--not quite closed or open--stared once again and started to dilate. Sillack walked back over to the ruby.

"If I remember my old friend, he was always weak, so it would not require strength to remove this jewel from its resting place."

The end of the eye

Hearing Sillack refer to Lackshin as weak grabbed Taddayuse's attention. He looked at

Sillack with great disgust. As a boy, Taddayuse grew up hearing of the hero Lackshin, and how he saved the lands from the same creatures he was there to help release. The wizard noticed his disapproving look at what Sillack had to say about Lackshin's strength. Still looking on, the boy wondered how he was to remove the ruby that earlier alluded the mighty Sillack. And he was soon to see what was to happen to this mystical jewel that was held by nothing and spun on its own axis.

Sillack being bent on obtaining the power that this ruby held, reached out his hand and placed it under the ruby that had now stopped spinning. He slowly raised his hand under it and gently pulled it free. The ring of water and fire now with no ruby ceased to exist. The once again exhausted wizard fell back on to Taddayuse--drained of his powers. The warrior stepped away allowing him to fall to the ground. Sillack turned with the ruby in hand, his eyes as well as the ruby glowing a blood red. The old warrior lowered his head in a disappointed manner and relaxed his grip on his sword because to him all was lost. As for Taddayuse, he looked at Sillack and for the first time saw him for what he really was. He was not the brave man who fought alongside Lackshin, but standing before him was a desperate man who would do anything to stay in power and retain his rule over the land. This man before him is going to release the biggest threat this world had ever known. The same creatures that kept the young Taddayuse up as a child are now again going to threaten the land. The Xyles that were free to dwell in the forest and protected the ruby's eye all suddenly went quiet. They each one by one made their way out into the clearing amongst Sillack's men.

"Men stand fast!" Shouted Fillip as he regained his grip of his sword.

Taddayuse turned to see what form of distress his friend was in. He turned to see the men not surrounded, but infested by the Xyles. The young warrior ran over to Fillip's side to join the fight alongside them.

"Put your swords down!" shouted Sillack

"These creatures that stand among you are now a part of my army; they are you, at least welcome them."

The men looked around in fear and uncertainty not knowing what to do. The Xyles stood among them with their chest pulsating and drool dripping from their fangs; not yet dry blood from the men they killed not so long ago in their earlier attack. Suddenly from the cave behind Sillack came the most blood curdling sound the men had ever heard. It was the awakening roar of a 1,000 or 10,000 Xyles, all coming to the surface to soon accompany their awaiting companions. The once swelling eye of fire and water came to a concentrated beam of still fire and water and returned to the ruby from whence it came; releasing a blanket of evil that at that moment covered the land.

Chapter Eleven

Feeling his blood turn cold, he settles himself in his chair. A cold breeze gently touches his cheek, "Did you feel that?" an alarmed Sanch asked. The scraping of the chair across the wooded floor echoed through the house. He sprang to his feet as he reached for his sword. "What was that?" He turns to see what could have touched him. "Did anyone feel that?"

"Yes and there is a strange familiarity to it." Ralyn replied.

"The feeling I have never felt before; some kind of evil," Bethany uttered, while looking aimlessly at Sanch.

Sanch still making his way to his sword still felt the cold touch the others did not feel.

"I have never felt such evil before. It was like it was trying to consume me, and everything around me. What manner of evil could that have been to make me feel such a manner?" Sanch replied, as he reclaimed his seat. "We must leave now. Alshin and the small army that rides with him cannot be too far from the village! We must try and stop them before they have the chance to make it here."

"You said a small army?" a confused Bethany inquired as she now rose from her chair. "When I saw this army you were speaking of come to think of it, it seemed like they were waiting for something. They might have been waiting for more men, as far as we know they could be 500 or 5,000 strong by now and on their way here as we speak."

A loud bang filled the room as Lisha slammed her hand on the marble table. "That scout I saw was not looking for us. He was riding off to take word to Sillack to have him send more men to reinforce Alshin and his forces. I should have known it would not be that easy. We should have killed him." Jumping to her feet now, Lisha grabbed her weapons and headed to the door.

"Where are you going?" Kess asked an almost running Lisha.

"I'm going after Sanch's old friend, Alshin."

That was enough to bring Menis to his feet, and on his way behind Lisha. Grabbing his axes he also made his way to the door.

Bethany and Sanch with weapons in hand the two of them still trying to shake the heavy dose of evil they were just overwhelmed with. Sanch with his sword strapped to his hip, and his father's sword in hand, he stopped and turned.

"I want to thank you for the meal. And know this: I will not let any harm come to you and your home or anyone here in this village, even if that means giving my own life to keep that promise."

As Sanch approached he noticed the door was open and Lisha, Bethany and Menis were just standing right outside the doorway. And over them was a strange shadow. Seeing that and not sure what was going on, Sanch started running for the doorway.

"What is going on?" Sanch shouted!

He ran through with no hesitation ready to take on whatever was on the other side of that door. Sanch, coming out in such haste, was forced to come to an immediate stop. Towering over them looking down at the four of them was Shallin with a look of disappointment on her face.

"Sanch, you are coerced to be in such haste to get to Alshin and his men."

"Who is out there?" Rayln shouted, as he emerged out of the house.

Not far behind were Thrant and Kess. Seeing what was going on and not being quite sure why.

"What is a dragon doing outside my home?" Kess asked as she pushed her way past the kids.

"I'm sorry," Sanch replied. "This dragon is here for me, she is called Shallin; the soul of my father's sword I think. I'm not quite sure just yet where she fits in with all of this. I think she is here to warn us of something." Sanch turned to Shallin for conformation on what it was he was claiming.

Before Kess stood Shallin a dragon whose scales were a reddish orange with a hint of green that showed, depending on the direction of the sun. Her eyes were haunting purple that glared right into your soul. The stronger she felt about what she was saying, or the angrier she was the redder her scales would glow almost to the point where you could no longer look upon her.

"Yes, you are correct young Sanch, you are all in grave danger. All the lands will be in peril if you are unable to stop the evil that will soon be upon us. There is great evil and power being directed straight at you, and bent on destroying you and I Sanch for we are the only ones who can stop them. And those who stand with you will make sure we get close enough to Sillack to end him."

Looking over to Lisha, Bethany and Menis, she continued, "With the help of the three loyal friends at your side victory will be yours."

"What manner of evil are you speaking of?" the young Sanch questioned the mighty Shallin.

Ralyn walked over to Lisha and Bethany. He stood proud behind them placing his large yet gentle hands on their shoulders. Menis, taking in all that was being said, griped tightly to his ax and gave Shallin his undivided attention, hanging on her every word.

"Sanch, two of your father's strongest adversaries have joined together to finish what was left undone eight years ago. They have put together an army of great magnitude, an army that will ravage through this land killing everything and everyone in its path, leaving death and destruction as far as the eyes can see. They will only stop if one of two things is accomplished."

"And what are those two things Shallin?" young Sanch asked, bravely stepping forward.

Shallin stood there with the look of despair in her eyes. Sorry that such a task is passed down to such a young man. A task she prays does not do to him what it did to his father.

"Sanch, they will not stop until we stop them, or until you and I are both no more. And those are the only two things that will bring this all to an end. Then there will be no one to stand between them and a reign of terror over all the land and its people. That is why we cannot let them succeed: we have to stop it this time at all costs."

"And that we will," replied Menis as he stepped to Sanch's side.

"And with friends like you three at his side I have no doubt that this land will be protected and kept ever safe from harm."

After saying that and seeing that the son of her old friend was well on his way to being just like if not greater than his father, that made it possible for her to fly away knowing she was leaving him with friends. Friends that would stand at his side and fight to the death against this evil he must face, but thank the Gods he is not alone. Shallin put down her head and spread her wings, throwing them straight up and coming down with a powerful force, giving off surprisingly a gentle breeze not an aggressive gust of wind. Lifting her gracefully from the earth taking her soaring up to the heavens, a stunning beauty. Left standing there was a boy who wanted nothing more than to bring a swift end to this evil and make it so that no one was harmed. Lisha, Bethany and Menis were nothing less than ready to follow Sanch to fight whatever evil he was to face on his quest.

"When do we leave Sanch?" asked Bethany. "We don't have that much time before Alshin and his men will be at our village gates. The people of this village can fight a small force, but if they all make it here I'm not sure if we will be able to stop them."

Bethany was correct; they had to do something and it had to be soon, the sun was falling rapidly towards the destined hills, soon to be behind them. The evening sky was bringing nothing but darkness with it. Everyone agreed, yet Kess found it hard to let her Bethany go with Sanch and the others. Kess knew that Bethany could take care of herself, but how dangerous would this be? How well will these four young warriors defend against Alshin and his trained army?
Kess grabbed her and pulled her off to the side. "Bethany must you go with them, can you not just tell them how to get there?"

"Wife, I know how you feel, but if she does not go with them they will have no chance of getting to Alshin in time to do anything to slow them down. Kess, I don't want her to go, but it is her turn to protect this village—her village, her home. We had our turn, let her have hers; she needs to go. She's her mother's daughter, she's a warrior," Ralyn said, embracing Kess while moving the hair from hiding her face, then gently kissed her on her forehead.

"Mother, don't worry I have my chosen Lisha to protect me."

Hearing that, Sanch turned and looked at Bethany. Noticing Sanch's interest in what she was saying she added, "Yes I almost forgot that I also have Menis there to keep me safe."

"Come on we must hurry we have no time to spare."

Closely following behind was Lisha and Menis heading to the gates that allowed them to exit the village.

"Thrant, what are you going to do to prepare the village against the men who make it to the gates?"

"Don't you worry young Sanch, we have protected this village before and we will do it once more." replied Ralyn. "Bethany is not the only warrior in this village; we will be ready for them when they get here, trust me. Now run off and catch up with the rest of your army. And Sanch make sure to bring them all back for we will need you all to ward off Alshin and his men."

"Sanch!" Kess shouted. "Please bring my warrior home to me. Now go and keep your promises to me and the people of this village."

"Trust in Shallin, Sanch. She as well as the others will be at your side when you most need them," Thrant shouted to Sanch as he ran to catch up with the others.

Kess turned to Ralyn. "Husband, what will they encounter in that dark forest?"

"I do not know Kess, I do not know."

Bethany took the others out to the end of the village where they could pick up some of her father's horses to ride. The reason they had to ride her father's horses was that they could find their way back to the village without riders; and they were the only horses that could be ridden bareback. Saddled horses could get caught on anything. Bethany informed the others that there would come a time on the path where they would have to go on by foot and the horses would have to be sent back to the village for if they were to stay in one spot they would most likely be eaten by the creatures of the forest.

She also told them of some of the strange things they might encounter on their travels through this mystical forest. Bethany had traveled this path several times prior to this but something was wrong. The forest seemed heavier to her somehow. She sensed another presence, a presence she had never felt before, but she thought nothing of it as she kept her mind on the task at hand. The four rode on, plus one Bethany did not know. Sanch also felt a presence but it was a presence he had felt almost longer than he could remember but it seemed much clearer to him now. Yet he did not quite understand why or what it was—it was as though the presence comforted him in his times of need. The ride to the part of the forest where they would have to send the horses back was not that long of a ride, but in their haste they made the journey even shorter. As they rode, Lisha noticed movement in the trees above them and quietly signaled to the others to stop. When doing so, the movement in the trees stopped as well. She brought them in closer and made it seem as if she were showing them something.

"Have any of you noticed any movements in the trees?" Lisha inquired.

"I have noticed sounds and movement but I have not seen anything," Menis replied.

Earlier Bethany noticed a presence and put the two together. The presence she felt must be what Lisha is speaking of.

"I have felt a strange presence since we left the village; this must be what you are seeing in the trees."

"It's just an old friend of ours Lisha, its nothing to be worried about; it's on our side. It is here to help if and when we may need it."

After Sanch said that, they all looked up into the trees and not too far above them was the creature looking at them as if to ask, "Why did we stop?"

The warriors all agreed since there was no reason to be fearful of this creature they should welcome his help and press on. As they pressed on Sanch began to wonder why it was that they could not ride the horses all the way to Alshin and his army. He was sure that would save them some time on their journey. Just then Bethany brought her horse to a stop, and the others did just the same, they had no choice. The others looked on not too sure of what they were looking at, or for. But Sanch at that point knew just why the horses had to go back at this point. All four got down from their horses: Lisha, Sanch and Menis knew not how they were to go on.

"Home!" shouted Bethany as she pointed the horses in the direction of the village where they would be safe.

Almost unnoticed their friend from the tree came to the ground next to Sanch and looked on with the others. Before them was the largest thorn forest they had ever seen. The vines stood at least four stories high and they went on for miles. The thorns were large enough to impale a grown man twice over, these thorns were the size of swords some of them even larger. From what Sanch and the others could see there was no way to get past this new obstacle.

"How are we to get past the thorns without being impaled by them?" Sanch questioned Bethany as he tested the sharpness of a close by thorn.

"We are not going through the thorn forest, we are going another way," she said with a mischievous smile.

"Oh, I see; so it is that simple, if I knew you could fly I would not have been so worried over how we were to pass," Sanch sarcastically replied.

"Now really, how are we going to pass?" Sanch once again questioned this time less patiently.

"Follow me," Bethany said, as she started off toward the right of the thorn forest.

"The path we will be taking to get past the forest is this way. I'm sure you know now how the village stays so safe against attacks. This thorn forest however so bothersome, but it keeps enemies and army's from attacking from this direction. We stay prepared but it is unlikely that we will have an attack from this direction."

"What is keeping the other side of your village protected from attacks?" Menis asked.

"You might find this hard to believe but the other side of the village there is a lake that is being fed by a strange waterfall coming from a hole in a mountainside," she said, as she lead the others through the now dark and dangerous forest.

"How is that so unbelievable? A lake being fed by a hole in a mountain; I can believe that," Sanch commented.

"That is not all," Bethany relayed. "That lake is why no one can enter our village from that side. For nothing can stay afloat on the lake, everything—and I mean everything sinks."

"So, what you are saying, that not even a man on a boat could cross this lake?"

"If you were to drop a leaf on this lake Menis, it would sink. Many men have died trying to cross this lake to get to our village; and none has yet to make it. Therefore I have faith that my village is safe," Bethany said, realizing what she had said quickly adjusted her previous statement. "Our village, Lisha's and mine--will be well defended from attack."

"So what you are saying?" Sanch added. "That there is no way for an army of any kind can get past that lake. That is the most incredible thing I have ever heard."

"This, coming from a boy with a pet such as the likes of that," Lisha said jokingly, as she ran her hand through the fur of the beast.

The giant creature let out a gentle growl in response to Lisha's touch. They pressed on still making good time on their journey. As they made their way toward the other side of the forest the creature grabbed Bethany by the shoulder as she was leading the group. Using his other arm he held Sanch and the others back. Menis being the warrior that he was drew his axe.

"What's going on?" Lisha asked as she went for her sword.

"Stop," Sanch whispered back to Lisha and Menis.

"He heard something. Be quiet and listen; there is something out there."

The warriors stood still and moved only to breathe; they made no sound. Where Sanch was standing he could see his protector's ears panning back and forth trying to pick up a sound and his nose flaring to and fro trying to pick up a scent. Then all of a sudden he jumped up and out into the dark of the forest. Then there was once again silence; they all stood there not quite knowing what to do.

"Look, what is that?" Bethany asked as she pointed into the forest where the creature had just disappeared. Coming toward them was a faint blue light. Bethany stood ready with her bow, Menis with his axe already drawn. Both Lisha and Sanch saw reason to join. They both drew their swords, Sanch from habit drawing his sword, leaving Shallin holstered wrapped in a blanket slung over his back. Then something strange happened. Sanch's sword became too heavy for him to hold onto and he then dropped it blade down, sinking halfway into the ground at his feet. Menis seeing what had happened with his axe ready put himself between Sanch and whatever was approaching from the forest.

"Stop!" Shouted Sanch. "It's him!"

Just as he said that the shadow of the creature broke through the darkness like glass. Coming from his hands was a faint blue glow. Just as a pet would bring its bounty to his master so did the creature to Sanch. He took one knee in front of Sanch as everyone gathered around to see what he was holding. He opened his hands and in them laid a blue glowing spirit that appeared to be injured.

"Is it okay?" Lisha asked the creature as she reached to touch it.

He looked up at Lisha and shrugged with a sad look on his face.

"Is there anything we can do to help it?" Menis franticly asked the others.

Putting away her bow, Bethany stepped forward. "Here, let me see if I think I can help."

"What are you going to do, what do you know about helping spirits?" Sanch asked as he stepped back to make room for Bethany so that she could get to the injured spirit. As she moved closer, the creature presented his hands to Bethany. She took the injured bearer of blue light from Sanch's protector and closed her hands around it until almost no blue was seen.

"What are you going to do with it?" Menis asked.

Turning to Lisha, Bethany signaled for her to come closer. "Lisha, come let me show you something that our grandmother taught me. She said this is something that all the females in our family can do."

"So what must I do to help?" an eager Lisha asked her cousin.

"Place your hands over mine and focus your energy to the tip of your fingers. Now concentrate on helping this spirit over everything; at this point and time nothing else matters. That is all you must think of...for this to work."

With their eyes closed Lisha and Bethany focused all their energy on the little spirit. The blue light now overwhelmed by the white light radiating from the two cousins hands. Both Sanch and Menis moved in closer to see what was taking place. The creature, Sanch's protector, still on one knee looked on as this spirit was once again made whole. The light grew brighter and brighter until the whole forest was engulfed in their healing white light, then suddenly the light was no more.

"Open your hands Lisha and you will see the gifts you have inherited; soon you will be able to do this on your own. Now look at what you have done."

Bethany opened her hands and from them came no longer a dim, but a bright glow of blue. A light shot from her hands straight up until it looked as to be among the stars. The creature sprung to his feet and like the others looked to the stars to see what would occur. The blue light slowly descended down to the shoulder of the strong yet gentle creature; her rescuer her hero.

"Thank you," they heard in a gentle whisper.

The creature nodded and answered with a growl.

"What do you mean it was nothing? If it were not for you that wild boar would have had its way, and I would no longer be. Instead you brought me to these two witches so that they could make me whole. That they did."

"Witches? We are not witches." Lisha replied.

"I do know that thought had entered my mind once before about you Lisha." Sanch jokingly added.

"What we did spirit was take something from ourselves and give it to you; healing your wounds. Just a little gift passed to us and we shared with you. So what is it that happened to you putting you in such a state?" Bethany asked the spirit now perched on the creatures shoulder.

"I was flying low looking for acorns to take back for my people. Acorns are a food we spirits enjoy eating. And I was out getting some when I was attacked by the wild boar. He nicked one of my wings making it hard for me to fly and keeping me low. May I ask you what business do you four and this extraordinary creature have in my forest?" The spirit asked Bethany.

"You young witch, I have seen you before traipsing through my forest but never have I ever seen you in such haste before. What is it that is chasing you, or is there some task you must accomplish in a timely manner?"

"We must get to the other side of this forest in a hurry as there is an army that will soon be marching to the village that these two call home," Sanch stated to the spirit.

"Then I can help you do that. It is the least I can do for the ones who restored me to health and gave me back my glow. This is my forest and I might be able to show you a shorter way out of here. Keep heading the way you were going and I will return to my people and let them know that I will be assisting you on your journey. I will meet up with you shortly; I will not be long."

Immediately after saying that she flew away leaving a stream of light in her wake; returning back into the forest leaving the four young warriors to ponder what had just taken place.

"Do you think she will return and do as she said?" Menis asked the others.

"I do not know, but if she does return, then her assistance would be very welcomed." Sanch replied. "And if she can help us get to Alshin's army any quicker, then that will increase our chances of defeating them or at least slowing them down, giving the village more time to prepare. Time may make the difference between winning and losing against Alshin's army."

"So let us do as she suggested and keep moving, if she comes back, then good. If not then we did not lose much time and we will just go the way Bethany had intended."

All being in agreement, they continued on toward the army bent on destroying Sanch and his father's sword.

Chapter Twelve

The heavy weighing on his shoulders, Sanch carrying the weight of both his and his father's sword as well as the weight of the village and it's people. His father's sword wrapped and strapped securely to his back as he kept his trusted sword close on his hip. They pressed on getting closer and closer to the path that would take them around the thorns. It seemed to take forever probably due to Sanch's eagerness.

"Are we getting closer Bethany?" Sanch asked, as he adjusted the sword strapped to his back, it was uncomfortable. "It seems as if our spirit will not be joining us on this journey after all, she must have found more pressing things to tend to."

"I guess we are on our own, no matter-- Bethany will get us there just the same. Plus I find my family more trust worthy then some spirit I know nothing about. So let's hurry and get to Alshin before he comes to us."

"No, it is not much further Sanch," Bethany answered. "It is right this way."

She took a few more steps to a clearing where they faced a large mountainside that seemed to go straight up. Lisha, Sanch and Menis looked at this mountain; knowing what they had to come to next. They had to start climbing, they did not know much of this land but they could tell that the army was on the other side of this mountain. And if they were to get to them and stop Alshin from killing innocent people they would have to climb to the other side. The three eager warriors started to do just that. Securing their weapons and the rest of their things the three started to climb.

"What are you guys doing?"

"Is this not the way we need to go? It seems to be the only way," Menis said as he stopped his climb.

"No, there is another way to make that journey," Bethany pointed to an opening between the mountain and the thorn forest. "Over there is the way we will take. This path will take us to another path in the mountain and bring us out behind Alshin's army. That should give us the element of surprise, and that would be the last thing that Alshin would expect to happen. The four of us showing up to the party early."

"Well, if that is so then let us be on our way; time is one thing we do not have a lot of," Sanch said as he walked toward Bethany's path. "If this is the way then let us be on our way."

"That is one way you can take, but by far it is not the best way nor is it the fastest way." They heard a voice coming from the forest. A blue light moved their way. It was the spirit with a much stronger glow than when they first met.

"Good of you to join us little one. I was starting to think you were not going to show up," an annoyed Lisha replied.

"Are you saying that you have a better way in which to get us on the other side of this mountain?" Bethany asked the spirit as she moved closer to better hear her.

"And which way would that be? If not over and if not around, then the only other way would be through the mountain and I do not see that happening," a skeptical Lisha added.

The spirit, seeming to be different then before, came out to join the others in the clearing. She was dressed in what seemed to be armor and she also had a bow over her shoulder with arrows in a bag, and a sword strapped securely to her hips. This spirit was dressed for battle, and battle is what she would see if she joined Sanch and the others. She will be apart of this quest that has united these four young warriors together for one cause, with one creature that seemed obligated to making sure to keep safe the son of Lackshin.

"You are dressed differently. Why is that?" Menis asked.

"Are we not going into battle?" The spirit asked, confused in response to Menis.

"Yes there is a fight waiting for us on the other side of this mountain, but you are just here to show us a quicker way to get there," Sanch added.

"I am here to help in anyway possible, even if that means fighting alongside you. My people live in this forest too and I plan on helping defend it. We are warriors just as you are, and are ready to defend our world."

"I am no longer going to argue with you!" Sanch firmly made clear. "You are right, this is your forest as well as the people of her village, and if you are willing to fight then who am I to stop you. We welcome your help in any way. But if you are to join us what are we to call you, what is your name little one?"

"I am called Silma," she proudly made known. "And I am here to fight at your side for if it were not for the two witches I would be no more." Flying over to Lisha and Bethany she said, "I owe you two my life and I intend to pay that debt to you both."

"So which way are we going?" Sanch asked once again. "Time is not something we have a lot of, so we need to get moving."

Silma turned to Sanch. "Through the mountain of course, that is the only other way we could go. Isn't that right, as she smiled at Lisha"

"And how are we to do this? It is not like there is a door on the mountain's side, and none of us here can walk through rocks," Menis pointed out to Silma.

"There is a door and my people are the ones who put it there. Back in my kingdom when I was preparing to join you I asked my father for the spell to open this door. And I will try and open it for us to pass through," Silma said, trying to reassure Menis with her plan to take them through the mountain.

"Stand back every one; I'm going to split this mountain in half now."

Silma flew over to the creature and took position in his large hands. From there she started to speak words that were foreign to the others, but seemed to be known by the creature. The blue that once surrounded Silma started to go from bright blue, then pink then green, and so on until it was almost impossible to tell what color she was at any given time. She glowed so brightly it engulfed nearly the creature's whole beauty with her radiance. Suddenly, the side of the mountain started to glow in reaction to Silma's power. Then there, through the colors was the door into the mountain of which Silma spoke. The door that would then take them to Alshin and his men.

"This way guys, hurry through the door as it will not stay open long. It will close as soon as we go through," Silma said hurrying them on.

"Come on!" shouted Sanch as he ran to the door. He wanted to waste no more time. His goal was to get to the other side of the mountain, and to Alshin for they had unfinished business. Following not too far behind him were Lisha, Bethany and Menis just as eager to face the battle that certainly awaited them on the other side. When they were all through, the spirit and the unnamed creature that held her and her power followed swiftly behind them. They now stood in a dark room with only the light from Silma to light their way.

"What now?" Bethany asked. "It seems to me like there is no where to go."

"But there is a way," Silma replied, and then uttered more words in her spirit tongue. There before them was a path lit by glowing rocks in the direction in which they needed to go.

Now perched on Sanch's shoulder, Silma gave her answer. "This is the way we must take. This will lead us to the other side. It will not take us long to reach the other side if we hurry."

After that was said they were on their way with much haste. As they made their way through the mountain they began to talk of the origin of this path.

"How did this place come to be? What reason would your people have to make such a big pathway through this mountain? It would make more sense if it was a smaller path more fitting for your stature," Menis pointed out.

"What I was told was that we were not the ones who needed this path through this mountain, that it was done as a favor for a great man with an equally important quest. This man also had a battle that awaited him on the other side. My father said there was something about this man that made him eager to help him in anyway he could. This man and his small band of men were heading to fight a battle in which they would be highly out numbered, yet they, just like you were eager to face their enemies. He was said to have had a very powerful sword, in which my father had never seen the likes of before. He said this sword had a black blade that strangely enough shined darkly."

Silma now had Sanch's full attention, it sounded to him like she was speaking of his father.

"And what was this man's name?" Sanch asked.

"He was called Lackshin, it was said that he would save us all from the evil that was sweeping over the land. And by the looks of things he did just that and we are all still thankful for that. Why do you ask Sanch; have you heard of him as well?"

"Silma, that sword on his back that sits not too far from you is the same one that your father spoke of. And the shoulder you sit on is that of Sanch the son of Lackshin," Lisha announced, making Silma aware of with whom she was traveling. "And his father gave his life making sure that the world remained safe from that evil. Now you Silma, have joined a quest to stop a new evil that now threatens these lands again, and you will now fight alongside the son of Lackshin." With a joking smile Lisha added, "I hate to say it, but that is something you can be proud of."

Sanch, hearing what was said, began to feel a little more relieved knowing that Lisha had some faith in him and the quest that he was on.

"You are right Lisha," Menis added. "And he is not too bad to have around when you are in a tight jam. And he is not too bad with a sword I might add."

"Well I have not known him for too long but from what I have seen he seems to know what he is doing."

"Well thank you Bethany; that means a lot to me, I will try my best to not let you or your village down. And I am sorry to have brought my fight to you and your people, this is my quest and I should have not involved so many of you." Sanch said as he lowered his head.

"I know that I have just joined your quest, but I am sure just like me, if they did not see your quest a just cause, that they would have not joined you. Besides, I think that this fight of yours will at the end involve many more then us. This is a fight that will take all who wish to have peace in these lands to win--led by you, the son of Lackshin. That will almost insure our victory. And Lisha is right; I am proud to have the honor to fight at your side and at the side of the three that accompany you on your quest. And not to mention this gentle yet powerful creature that seems not to leave your side for any reason."

"Well I pray to the Gods that I do not let you all down. I am not my father yet I am here to finish what he had started, and with you all at my side I think I can do just that. So tell me Silma, how much further on until we are on the other side of this mountain? It seems like we have been walking for hours and still we are not killing Alshin or his men as yet. I am getting just a little anxious that's all."

"Silma, how is it that your father was able to get Sanch's father and all his men through, and it barely stayed open long enough to get six of us through, why is that?" curiously Bethany asked the spirit.

"My father is much more powerful than I. If he wanted, he could leave it open as long as he wanted to. That is what took me so long to return to you from the spirit city. I had to learn the words to speak in order to open the path through the mountain; as you can see, it took a lot out of me. My father could do the same with little to no effort; that is how he was able to keep the mountain open long enough to let Lackshin and his men through to the other side."

Just then, Sanch came to a stop and signaled to the others to do the same.

"Why did we stop?" asked Silma as she flew off his shoulder to get a better look at what was going on.

"There is something in here with us, I can hear it breathing and it knows we're here."

Sanch's protector then reached up and gently closed his hand around Silma, closing in her glow.

"That's a good idea--now whatever is in here with us will not be able to see us."

"Yes, that is good, but how are we to see our way out of here?" Bethany whispers to Sanch as she reached for her staff.

"Silma, how well do you know this mountain?" Lisha asked the captive spirit.

"Well enough to get us through in the dark," she replied. "And besides we spirits can see in the dark almost as well as we can see in broad daylight, so don't you worry young witch, we will be just fine."

"I would still recommend we keep our weapons ready, we still do not know what we might be up against," Sanch whispered. "This thing is still coming and I don't think it is too far away, so I think we should make haste."

"Yes, we should be on our way," Silma agreed, then let out a small thin beam of light through the creature's hand in the direction they needed to go. And with weapons in hand they preceded in the direction the spirit designated.

Menis, with axe in hand turns to Sanch, "I guess this is the way we must go."

"She has not led us wrong thus far, so I do not see a reason to think that she is going to start now. So, yes I guess this is the way we must go, and I hope we will be the only ones going that way. We should hurry the faster we are out of here the better. If we do not have to face this creature, we will be much better off, so let us hurry for our battle lay on the other side of this mountain."

And they did just that, haste was made. They took up a slow run to quicken the journey to the other side. The whole time being pressured by some kind of unknown creature with intentions they knew not of. Sanch was able to keep track of the creature by listening to it's breathing as well as its heart beating in anticipation. They were clearly being hunted by this thing, and it was getting closer. Menis, being the warrior that he was, noticed something that the others including Sanch did not notice.

"Sanch, how many of these things did you say were after us?"

"One. Why do you ask Menis? Is there something else?"

"Yes, I do not think it is alone, I think it is one of many. In fact, I think the one that is close to us is only a scout and the others are not too far behind. And I do not think we are going to want to be here when the others arrive and we must hurry; there is no time to waste." Saying that, they picked up their pace. They wanted to make sure not to get trapped in the mountain with whatever creature or creatures that may mean them harm. Even in their haste, they still were not able to make it to the other side without confrontation, for they were there at the exit waiting for them. They were now surrounded and these things were now both behind as well as in front of them.

They had no choice now but to fight if they were to ever leave the center of this mountain. The four young warriors with weapons in hand stood ready for whatever was stalking them in the dark. The creature that had joined them still had Silma in the palms of his hands where she was building up her powers for the upcoming confrontation. She figured she might have to open the path out of the mountain in a hurry, or they might all be lost. Sanch signaled the others to come in closer; he had something to say to them.

"Form a circle around him and get ready for what we might see when the lights come on."

Sanch turned to the creature, "You wait for my signal and you will know what to do."

The creature nodded in understanding of Sanch's order. They now stood still in formation around the creature facing outward toward the approaching danger. Now still they were all able to hear what it was that both Menis and Sanch already knew. They could hear the movement of these things around them.

"How many of them do you think is out there Lisha?" Bethany whispered to her cousin.

"I don't know but it sounds like more then we are going to be able to handle, but that's what makes it so much fun. I just hope Sanch has a plan that's not going to get us all killed."

Just then he made his plan known.

"Now!" shouted Sanch. "Now!"

In a matter of seconds, the whole cave was illuminated with Silma's magical glow. Hovering over the four heroes she shot four arrows and planted them right in front of Lisha, Bethany, Menis and Sanch; giving them what light they might need to ward off whatever might come out from the darkness.

There in the dark were what looked to be two glowing eyes glaring back at them. Slowly the creature that belonged to those eyes stepped out to show himself. There, standing before them was a green scaly man like creature and behind him he dragged a thick powerful tail that he seemed to have full control over. Sanch, knowing Lisha's style of doing things, kill and ask questions later, reached over and placed his hands on her shoulders. Just in time to stop her advance.

"Stand down, I do not think it means us any harm, but do not for a minute let your guard down. That goes for all of you. Let's hear what it might have to say."

"Where are the rest of them? There were more of them, he is just the scout, the others are still out there. We should very much stay ready; we do not know what their intentions may be," Menis added.

"Yes he is right, stand ready." Sanch agreed.

Just then, the strong center of their circle let out a roar and jumped past the protection of Silma's bright glow into the darkness still above them all.

"What is he doing?" Bethany shouted. "Were did he go?"

"I don't know cousin, just remain ready for anything."

Shortly after entering the darkness, he descended back to the center of his companion's defense, but he was not alone. With him he had one of the creatures that had been hunting them. He reached under his ripped garments and pulled out an unusual blade and held it to the creature's neck.

"Stop, do not hurt him; we mean you no harm. We did not know what to expect from you." The green stranger shouted, "Please do not harm him."

"You said you mean us no harm. Where are those that you travel with if I only see you and your friend here? If you do not want him dead, you should have them show themselves," Sanch said as he looked to his friend giving the nod to keep the creature at bay.

The stranger looked up and spoke out in his own strange tongue, and in reaction 30 of his men safely fell to the ground. Not liking what they saw, their comrade being held by blade pulled their weapons.

"Stop, we are not here to fight them!" he shouted.

"Then what are you doing here if not to fight?" Menis boldly asked.

"To offer my help and the help of my men, one of which you hold there on the ground. Now that my men are before you can you please let him return to his feet?" He said as he pointed to his man that was being detained. Getting the okay from Sanch, the creature was released, and allowed to join his comrades.

"Thank you for releasing him to me; we still mean you no harm. If you could please lower your weapons as I am just here to talk, and to offer my assistance and the assistance of my men."

Not sure of his motive, Sanch asked why. "What reason could you have to help us? You do not know of our quest. And why would you want to leave the safety of this mountain and put your people in danger? Do you have any idea what is unfolding outside this mountain? Before this is over, several people are going to die. And you and your people do not need to be among them; I have placed far too many people and their safety at stake, and I do not wish to add to that."

"Sanch, I do not know if you have noticed but when we leave this mountain we are going to be very outnumbered. He and his men might be just what we need to keep my village from getting slaughtered; we are going to need help."

"Bethany, what are you saying? We know nothing of them. Why am I to believe that they want to help us?"

"I assure you that my men and I wish to help; we mean you no harm," the stranger added as he made his way over to Sanch and his companions who had put away their weapons.

Even Silma had returned to the others on the shoulder of Sanch's protector and reduced her glow. It seemed that everyone including Silma agreed with what the stranger was offering; they all knew without him and his men they would be greatly outnumbered. Sanch on the other hand did not want to put what he felt were innocent people in the way of danger. Sanch was still consumed with the guilt of bringing Alshin and his men down on Bethany and her village and he was not ready to do that again.

"I am sorry but I had overheard there in the shadows the story that your spirit had told you, and it is similar to one I have heard. As a child my father told me of a great man who risked all to make the land safe from the evil that threatened it. He told me that this man carried a sword with a strange black blade that would cut through stone. This man stepped in just in time to save my father and our people from extinction and complete annihilation. The fight that went on between my people and the Xyles went on to a stalemate until they became more powerful then we could ever have imagined, and we began to see defeat where before we saw victory.

In the story my father said that our numbers began to diminish and even our women and children were being hunted and killed, and that was not something my father would allow. He had his men bring the women and children to this mountain and hide them inside to keep them out of harms way. Here where they would be safe from the claws of our enemies; the Xyles.

This way my people would have the opportunity to live on. But just as my father and his men were going to return to the fight they ran into a man. This man had a small army of men with him and they too were going to face an army of Xyles just as they were. At first just like us they almost went to battle with one another. No blood was shed but it came close. I was told that they were able to stop long enough for my father and this man to talk. They both realized they shared the same fight and enemies shared friends made, and the forces were joined and it was a great force, but not great enough. If it were not for the man they call Lackshin our whole army would have been lost and there would have been no one left to protect our people. Lackshin told my father to leave half of his army here and to take the other half into battle against the Xyles. And if it were not for that decision, we would have lost many more then we did."

"What do you mean, the Xyles were defeated along with the wizard that controlled them? Is that not how it happened; is that not how the story went?" Bethany reciprocated.

"Yes, they won but not without taking on a great number of lost. I do not know what you were told about that day, but that day was a bloody day. The battle was a fierce one and there were a lot of lives lost that day. My father left with 10,000 of his men and returned with a 167 men and 20 of them just made it back in time to die among their people. So yes, the battle was won but at a high cost, one that we are not again willing to pay."

"What do you mean, the Xyles have been unseen for many years, they are not the enemy we go to face."

Menis stepped forward, "We go to face the one called Alshin and his army that will soon be marching on Bethany's village if we don't stop them, or at least slow them down before they get there."

"The Xyles are once again free to ravish the land and we must stop them from doing so as they did long ago."

"That feeling that came over me like a great evil was suddenly among us," Sanch remembered.

"That evil you felt was the same that came over me; an evil that ran through my body. It was the greatest evil that will once again ravish the land if they are not stopped. And that is a battle that we will all have to fight before this is all over, and that is what I thought you were doing here. That is why we were following you. So I am sorry if we startled you in any way, that was not our intent," the stranger said with great remorse.

"If what you are saying is true, then we are going to need an army to go up against this force. And if these Xyles are as bad as you are saying, then I do not know if even an army is going to be enough," Lisha said, but in no way was that going to stop her from trying.

"It is going to have to be enough for we cannot allow those things to once again consume and destroy the land. If they are not stopped, no one will be safe; they will kill until no one is left. I only wish we had what my father had."

"And what is that?" Menis enquired.

"Lackshin of course, he is who saved my people from extinction," the stranger answered. "He is what we need to be victorious."

"No, we do not have Lackshin but we are not lost." Lisha said sounding reassured.

"What do you mean?" The green man asked.

Lisha answered with a familiar smirk on her face, "We have Sanch the son of Lackhsin, and he is just going to have to do. And Sanch, from what I have seen, is a great warrior and will finish what his father started. If you are to join us we are going to need to know what to call you."

"I am sorry I have not yet introduced myself, I am Deem, son of Esaab, the prince of the Elarguns. And the one you had in your custody for that short period of time, he is my brother, we call him Dagger."

"Why is it that you call him Dagger?" Menis wished to know.

"If he was not ordered not to harm you at any cost you would have known by now why he is called Dagger. Yet I am sure before all of this is over you all will know why," said Deem, trying to reiterate why it was so important to stop the Xyles. "My men and I are ready and prepared to stand at your side as our fathers stood next to yours so long ago. Some of our fathers did make it back and told us of the merciless fight they faced in battle agents the Xyles. They are said to be without fear. And they show no mercy to their enemies; nor will they spare the friends of their enemies and they will kill all who stand in their way--women and children the same--no one will be safe."

"How are we to defeat them if they are so powerful? What could have released them from their confinement? And how would someone go about releasing such creatures on the land and why would anyone do that knowing the kind of destruction they will cause," Silma asked.

"A desperate man with everything to lose--a man called Sillack. He has obviously been told that I am coming for him, or he would not have sent so many men with Alshin. He either wants me dead or brought to him. He fears my father's sword and what I can do with it. Sillack wants both me and this sword destroyed at any cost; that is why he would release such an uncontrollable evil on this world."

"All this to stop a boy with his father's sword. Why would he do all this just for a sword and this young boy, it seems too much." Dagger wondered out loud.

"Is this the kind of evil we are to face outside the safety of this mountain? If we are going to defeat this Sillack, we are going to need to take our best men if we are to have a chance at stopping his army of Xyles," Dagger added.

"What say you Deem? Are we to bring more men on this quest?"

"Yes Dagger."

"I want you to go back to Elargun city and bring more men, but make sure to leave enough to protect our city and the people in it."

"How are they to join us without the spirit to open the path through the mountain?"

"Bethany is right," Silma agreed.

"How are they to join us without me to open the mountain for them?"

"We have other ways out of the mountain, but it will take much more time before we would be able to join the fight. The sprits door has always been the fastest way out of the mountain." Deem said to Sanch.

Sanch stopped to think on the dilemma that was brought to him. He did not know how they were to join them as soon as they were needed without Silma. Because of his nature, Sanch did not fully trust Deem and his men and was not sure if it would be safe to leave Silma in Dagger's care.

"I will leave Silma with Dagger that way he can bring his army through Silma's doorway. That way it will not take long for them to join us in the fight."

"Sanch, do you think that is the solution; leaving Silma here with them? I mean what do we really know of them; we do not know their intentions to be true. They might even mean us harm," Menis said clearly.

"Menis is right; what do we know?" Lisha agreed.

Sanch turned to his strong but silent protector and reached up and put his hands on his shoulder.

"You both are right, that is why I am not leaving Silma alone, she will be in good hands. I am going to have my friend here accompany Silma back to the city with Dagger. I think we all will feel much better if that is done."

The silent giant nodded and reached his hands out to receive Silma.

"We mean you no harm and if this will show that to you, then I welcome him."

Dagger stepped forward to show that he concurred with what was being asked of them. "As do I, he is most welcome to join me and my men. And I am looking forward to becoming his friend as opposed to his victim. It will be my honor to show you both to my city and have you see how my people live and what we will be fighting for."

"Yes, but first she must let us out so that we can make our way to Alshin and his army. In fact, we should be going; we have wasted enough time," Sanch said as he turned towards the exit.

The 30 who stood with Deem and Dagger seemed ready and anxious to go through a new door. And now the concern was how long Silma would be able to hold the gateway open for 30 more than before, for when it was just five it left her exhausted. Sanch also was fearful that she may not have the ability to hold it open for the force that will be accompanying Dagger from the Elargun city, and if not, then how would they be able to join the rest?

"Silma, are you going to be able to hold the gateway open long enough to allow us all to pass through?" Bethany asked as she looked to their new allies. "You were weakened when you had only five, now there are 35 who must pass."

"I do not know, I was weakened but I feel with the help of you both it should seem not as difficult. That thing you two did for me back in the forest should give me the strength that I may need to keep the gate open both for 35 as well as the army that Dagger is saying he can produce."

"Lisha, Bethany, do it! We have no time to waste. We are going to need to have that gate open for us to be successful against Alshin's army," Sanch stated.

And they did just that--Lisha and Bethany took Silma into their hands once more and focused their energy this time to strengthen her as opposed to saving her life. The bright light returned and the energy was felt all throughout the mountain. Deem and his men stepped back from the light, for they had never felt such power. Both down on one knee, they opened their hands and released Silma into the air. Silma, full of energy and power repeated the words that will again open the mountain and release Sanch and his newly found allies.

Chapter Thirteen

The walls started to vibrate slowly almost giving off a quiet hum. Silma's new charge of power re-ignited the glowing rocks on the cave walls.

"Menis, Lisha, Bethany, you three lead them out and Deem and I will follow and make it quick, I want Silma to save her strength for the force that Dagger is to bring."

With her new power the gateway was opening much quicker than before. It was now opened just enough for some to pass through. Bethany being the smallest of the three went through first. And led the way with Lisha then Menis following close behind.

"Hurry men!" Shouted Deem, "Get through the gate there is no time to waste!"

Sanch stepped to the side with his protector, looking up at him giving him strict orders.

"Look over her with the same watchful eyes you use to look over and protect me."

He looked to Silma then back to Sanch, and nodded to show he understood. With that being said, Sanch followed Deem through the opening in the mountain, disappearing into the dark on the other side. Silma descended into the hands of her hero.

"Thank you, I know I'm in good hands and you will take care of me," Silma said as she looked into the creature's eyes who had sworn to protect her.

"Let us go." Dagger said. "Sanch is right, we do not have much time to stop the one called Alshin from destroying that village. It is imperative that we make it in time to help win this battle."

Now they were on their own and on their way to Elargun where the army was said to be waiting. The first few moments of the journey were quiet, no one was sure what could be said. Remember Dagger and Silma's friend first met with him holding a blade to his neck. Dagger felt he needed to gain the trust of Silma. Therefore Dagger spoke first.

"So friend, where did you get such an exquisite weapon like the one you used to hold me at bay?"

"He does not speak, he has not said a word since I encountered him and the others."

"Did I not see Sanch speak to him right before he passed through the gate?" Dagger asked.

"Yes he did. He may not speak but he seems to understand us just fine, and strangely enough I somewhat understand him."

"What is his name?" Dagger asked looking back and up at the silent giant.

"If I understand correctly he has not yet been given one."

"What does that mean? How could he not have been given a name?" Whatever he is—he is no child and must have a name. What does Sanch call him?"

"From what I've seen he calls him his protector, and that seems to suffice," said Silma as she flew ahead to take a look. And then back safely to the shoulder of her friend.

He nodded and seemed to smile.

"I can see why he would be called that, there is more to this creature then you know."

"What do you mean?" Silma asked.

Dagger, seeing first hand what the he was capable of, saw things not seen by the others.

"Have you noted that other than the light you produce there aren't any lights in these caves?

The reason for that is just like your friend we can see very well in the dark."

"How do you know he can see in the dark?" Silma inquired.

"Did you see me and my men on the roof of the cave?"

"No I did not, and nor did any of the others."

"He not only saw us, he chose me from the others; it was like he knew who I was. Not only that, when he left the ground I felt his presence twice, one that remained on the ground and the one approached me on the roof of that cave. I don't yet know what it is, but there is something about you my friend. Something powerful and unique, and that Sanch boy has something to do with the source of that power."

Just then they came to a stop, both drawing his weapons. There was something in the dark and it was moving toward them and it was fast.

"What is it?" Silma asked as she herself pulled her weapon.

The creature took Silma and gently pulled her in close to keep her safe. He was not going to let Sanch down. He put his dagger away and used both hands so he could better protect Silma. Dagger signaled for them to get down, he could sense them approaching but could not tell from what direction.

"Silma can you oppress your glow?"

"Yes. Why?"

"Just do it! They are getting closer! When I give you the word bring back the glow as bright as you can, these things don't like the light. Your glow should send them running back to the holes they came from."

They now lay waiting in the dark for these things that approached. Silma stood ready in the hands of now her protector waiting for Dagger to give the sign. The closer they got, the more you could hear their blood curdling squeals closing in on them.

"How many of them are there?"

"I don't know," Dagger whispered as he signaled to Silma to remain quiet.

Now at this point, the squeals were ear piercing and it was almost more than Silma could take, and not a moment to soon Dagger gave the signal knowing his silent friend would be able to hear him when he shouted.

"Now!"

The creature launched Silma into the air, and she took that as her clue to glow. Inches from his face Dagger could feel its breath. One of these things ready to devour anything in its path was almost on top of him. Silma radiated like the sun, bringing these creatures into a light they had never seen in their dark world. That gave Dagger just what he needed to go from the hunted to the hunter. With the light she gave, Dagger showed Silma just why he is called Dagger. He took the two daggers that he carried and with little to no effort dismembered the beast. Spilling its insides splashing it onto the cave floor. The others not able to function in such light turned bumping into one another. Just as fast as they came they went, and Silma returned to her normal glow.

"What were those things?" Silma asked as she flew over to get a better look at the one Dagger killed. "Why were they hunting us?"

"That is just what they do: hunt, kill and feed. Now let us go, it's not much further to my city. We need to hurry back to Deem, he is going to need me at his side, and that is where I plan to be. As you my friend, I am sure wish to be at Sanch's side."

Turning to Protector Dagger asked, "Are you going to be able to keep up; we're going to be moving fast from here on."

Donning a familiar smile he nodded, and pulled Silma in close once again where she would be safe. Then off they went into the darkness as they closed in on Elargun city, where Sanch's new army was stationed. The Elargun army was waiting for their captain who was on his way. On the outside of the mountain Bethany was dealing with Sanch and his impatience.

"Bethany, besides that large gate, what kind of defenses does your village have? I ask this in case we are not able to stop Alshin's army from reaching your village. I just need to know that your people in some way will be able to defend themselves until we make it to them." The son of Lackshin asked sounding very agitated.

"The people of my village are warriors and have before defended themselves, but the ones who have seen war no longer wish to fight. Then there are young men of the village trained for war but have never seen it. And after our mothers, Lisha's and mine, women were no longer trained to fight. If it were not for my father I would not have myself been trained to fight and track the way that I can. And there are other women of the village that came from worlds that our mothers lived in that can also fight. But I do not think you should worry. My father, I am sure at this time, is preparing the people in the village to defend themselves."

"Good then." Menis chimed in. "There is a chance that your village will survive this attack. And is that not why we just crossed through a mountain?"

"Hopefully with our combined forces we can stop this army well before it reaches this village you speak of, and all will be well." Deem said, making known that their goal of saving this village was now his goal as well.

"Deem, are you sure that Dagger and your army will make it in time?" Lisha asked.

"They ran into some trouble, but they are well on their way now and will be at my city shortly."

"And how could you know that?" A confused Sanch asked as he rubbed his head.

"Well son of Lackshin, my brother and I are very close."

"I see," replied Sanch as he signaled to pick up the pace.

They traveled the rest of the way in silence, all contemplating the battle yet to come. The four young warriors accompanied by Deem and his men, off to face a greater force than theirs even with their new allies. They knew they would still be greatly out-numbered, yet the only thing on their minds was the safety of the village. Bethany hoped that she was right and her father was preparing the people of the village to face an army that wished to exterminate them all in the name of Sillack. Ralyn being the man that his little girl knew him to be was diligently preparing his people. He brought all that were able to make it to the entrance of the village, and told them of the approaching danger they were soon to face. Some did not understand and others trusted Ralyn and were prepared to follow him through the fires of hell. The ones who did not understand still trusted him, but were filled with fear. Ralyn's job as leader was to elevate the fear that his people felt, as well as making sure the fires of hell did not destroy his village.

"Did the one who calls himself the son of Lackshin bring this upon us?" shouted a woman in the crowd.

"He is here to help us. This army had our village in its sights; he is here to make sure the peace that his father helped give us remains. Right now he and three others are on their way to face this army with not much chance of success. Know this, two of the three that accompany him are of my house. I have faith that he will not let us down, I believe he will stop them or at least slow them down enough to give us a chance to prepare."

"How much do you trust this boy, do you trust him with our lives?" again the women questioned Ralyn.

"My daughter Bethany is with him, so yes, I trust him with my life and so should you!"

Kess standing at her husband's side was growing highly impatient, she knew only one thing and that was Bethany was out there where it was not safe. She heard the dragon and knew of the danger her little girl could be facing, and she was not willing to have her face it alone.

"I have heard enough! My husband has said all he needs to say! The ones that will fight will stand at his side, and the ones who will not will go home and wait for death to come for them. We all have fought for peace before, and before the sun sets tomorrow we all will fight for peace again."

"She is right!" Shouted a young man from the crowd. "If they are coming we will have no choice but to fight if we wish to stay free."

"Thanks Evian. Will no one else stand and fight with me; or will Evian and I be the only two fighting for the fate of this village?"

To Ralyn's surprise there were more like Evian, young and old willing to fight at his side. Seeing that, Ralyn felt like his village might just have a chance and that took some weight off his shoulders. Ralyn then turned and started home.

"What are we to do now?" Evian asked.

Ralyn turned and placed his hand on the young man's shoulder.

"Evian go home and make your home and your family safe, and after you do so return here and we will make our village safe for us all."

"Why would you not secure the village first husband?" Kess asked not understanding.

"Kess, when a man's home and family is made safe he will fight that much harder to keep it that way. And his mind will be on the fight and that is how it needs to be if we are to win this fight. Now let us hurry and get back to the house so Thrant and I can try and come up with a way to keep us all alive."

"Why did Thrant not come with us to speak to the people; they are his people as much as they are yours."

"He has been away from them for a long time and does not yet feel that he has the right to ask them for any thing...much less to risk their lives."

"Do you really think we have a chance against this army?"

"We have Thrant, one of the best fighters that has ever come out of this village, and he came here for the purpose of protecting his home."

"Does he still consider this his home?" Kess asked.

"Yes he does, and he just like I, would die to keep it safe, this I know. And if all else fails, then there is Sanch. And, if he is anything like his father he will do just as he said: protect the people of this village from the enemy he feels he brought to these gates. And with what the dragon spoke of, I feel this will only be the first of many battles to come."

"Why is it that you would think such a thing?" Kess asked, worrying even more now about Bethany.

Not knowing just how to tell Kess of the real evil that has again been released, he hesitated then turned to his wife. "The evil that Sanch felt is an evil that at one time almost destroyed everything we held dear to us. The creatures that Sanch's father once put to rest some how have been set free."

"Are you telling me there are Xyles out there with my child Ralyn?"

Ralyn answered regrettably, "Yes, I am almost certain that is what he felt, and I'm sure the others felt it too. And never feeling such evil before, it had to have been overwhelming for the three of them."

"Ralyn, Sanch may be able to stop Alshin and Sillack, but do you think he will do the same when he is faced with an evil like the Xyles?"

"Well, if the son of Lackshin can't stop them then we are truly lost. Come on, let us at least try and save our village for now, and worry about the Xyles when they come." Ralyn replied and they continued home.

Chapter Fourteen

A breeze blew down from the nearby mountains blowing Kess's hair into her face. Ralyn stopped and looked at his beautiful wife standing there looking up at him through her thick black hair. He gently moved just enough of her hair to uncover her full pink lips. He leaned down and softly kissed her and in that moment all was right in the world. Ralyn was then nuzzled from behind. The two looked and to their pleasant surprise it was Gold, Gallop, Speed and Aly the fastest of the four; the horses that Bethany and the others rode out on. They were returning home just like Bethany said they would; they did know the way. Kess did not quite understand why the horses were returning to them without Bethany and the others.

"What are they doing here?" She franticly asked. "What does this mean? Does this mean they are…" She paused burying her face in Ralyn's chest. He put his arms around her and held her tightly.

"No my love," he said, "They are fine; they got to a point in the forest where the horses could no longer go, so they sent them back."

"So what you are saying is that the next time we see them they will be on the other side of an army? And what again were they going to do when they did catch up with this army?"

"I know now that we must be ready, for the most they can do against Alshin is slow him and his men down long enough to give us time to prepare, and I hope that we can."

Going from a fast walk to an all-out sprint, Kess and Ralyn took off toward their home. They got to the door and swung it open with great haste. Both shouting for Thrant, finding to their surprise he was missing. Ralyn instructed Kess to prepare herself as well as to retrieve his armor that he so hoped never to have the need for.

"Has he left us again? Now when we need him the most, his sword could mean the difference of victory or defeat for this village, his village, his home!"

"No Kess, I think I may know were he has gone. Do what I have asked of you and I will return with Thrant and his sword. Do not fret my love, this is not a fight we will lose, the warriors of this village will not allow that to happen. Not I, nor Thrant will let our home fall. The only fires will be flames of victory." And off to find Thrant he went on Aly with Gallop close behind.

The tough bark rough on his skin; running his hands up and down a tree still standing strong in spite of the abuse it received from his sword. Thrant stood in a clearing where he and Lisha's father spent several hours working on their skills with a sword; skills he was now not sure of. Was his enough to help keep Alshin's men from taking the village? Thrant knew first-hand the kind of evil that was coming and the destruction it would leave in its wake if not stopped. The thought of once again letting down these people, his people, was overwhelming.

"Will they fight?" Thrant asked.

"Yes," Ralyn responded. "They will fight and die if need be to protect their home."

"And so shall I fight to do the same," Thrant answered as he turned to Ralyn. "I see the horses have returned. I guess they made it to the thorn forest and are well on their way to catch up with the army."

"Yes and we must make sure that there is help waiting here for them when dawn comes." Ralyn said as he rode up next to his old friend.

"Are one of those horses for me or shall I run alongside?" Thrant jokingly inquired.

"Yes my friend; let us ride, we have a battle to win."

"Ralyn, I may not be much good to you for I have no true sword."

"That shall be remedied, let us ride."

Off they rode back to Ralyn's home to get Thrant a sword worthy of a warrior such as himself. Back at Ralyn's home Kess was preparing his armor, as well as preparing herself for battle. She pulled out her chest plate, both her and Ralyn had them well put away never thinking they would have reason to once again wear. In it were her twin crossbows that she had not used since before Bethany was born.

"A little dusty but they should still work just fine. I just hope I still remember how to use them."

Lying next to them was her sword, it still had its shine and was still as sharp as last she used it. It remained wrapped safely in cloth. She was hesitant to touch it. She knew if she did there would be no turning back and war was inevitable. In it were the garments she once wore to battle against the Xyles and the same garments she had still stained with blood. She so hoped she would never have to don them again. Kess, thinking of her daughter, Bethany, who was outside the safety of their wall's stopped hesitating and put on her old warrior garments. She discarded her dress that defined her as the wife of Ralyn the lord of the village, and now wore what made her his equal as a warrior. As she tied the straps on her boots, she felt a breeze creep in. The door opened behind her.

"Is that not what you were wearing when I fell in love with you?" Ralyn asked.

"It looks to me Kess as though you are ready for battle. And who will you be fighting?"

Trying to keep her warrior prestige, she turned and said, "Did you find Thrant?"

"Yes I did; he was right where I thought he would be. He was in the clearing where he and Kanten spent several hours hacking away at that tree with their swords."

"What was he doing there?"

"He like us, was gathering his strength from where he knew he would find it. Thrant mentioned to me that he did not have a sword, and I told him that there was one here worthy of him."

"And what sword did you have in mind Ralyn?" Kess asked inquisitively.

"I had his brother's sword in mind; since he no longer has the one we had made for him, Kenten's sword would be fitting."

"I'm glad you feel that way." Kess said as she turned to face her husband.

Ralyn confusingly asked, "Why is that?"

"Because Thrant's old armor and his brother's sword are both laying on the dinner table waiting for him. I thought that would please him," Kess said still gloating.

"I almost forgot something," Ralyn said as he pulled her to him.

"What is that husband?"

"I almost forgot that you were as smart as you are enchanting."

In the arms of her husband, Kess feels safe, but she still can't help but to worry about the approaching danger of Alshin and his army. The safety of Ralyn's arms may be enough for Kess but it will not be enough to keep the whole village safe from Alshin.

"Ralyn, do you think we will be able to stop Alshin from destroying our home, and if we stop him what then? What will we do if Sillack follows with an even bigger army?"

"We have no choice but to stop Alshin's army; we don't have the luxury of losing. If we cannot stop Alshin's force then what chance does the rest of the world have against Sillack? What chance would Bethany and the others have? That

feeling that came across Bethany and Sanch was
one all too memorable: the Xyles roaming
around free to reap destruction and carnage
behind them. If we do not give Sanch and Shallin
a chance to get to Sillack all will be lost—
Bethany could be lost, and we cannot allow
either to take place. Stopping them is the only
choice we have. Failure is not an option."
®

Watch for Heart of the Sword II, coming soon.

Cast of Characters

Sanch: son of Lackshin
Shallin: Sword of Lackshin
Helen: Saved by Sanch
Lisha
Vaness: Lisha's Mother
Thrant
Menis
Bethany
Silma: the Sprit
Kess (Kuess): Bethany's mom
Ralyn: Bethany's father
Hannes: Menis clansmen
Deem: Prince of the Elarguns, thirty men with him
Dagger: Deem's second
Esaab: Deem's father
Sillack: once known as Sill
Alshin: commander
Rinnis: horse-like creatures
Xyles: creatures
Haygen: Sillack's second
Taddayuse from Tegra
Fillip the old warrior
Daren: known as The Wizard
Evian: young man in Ralyn Village
The horses: Gold, Gallop, Speed and Aly